The frightening ....
engaged in a grisly search for the
inexplicable truth. It entangles them in
a chilling nightmare which does not
end when they wake up.

Sphere Books: the summit of original
science fiction

*Also by Jerry Sohl and available
in Sphere Books*

THE TIME DISSOLVER

THE ODIOUS ONES

The
Odious Ones

JERRY SOHL

SPHERE BOOKS LIMITED LONDON

Copyright © 1959 by Jerry Sohl
First Sphere Books edition, 1967

Canadian agent: Thomas Nelson and Sons
                     (Canada) Limited,
                     81 Curlew Drive,
                     Don Mills, Ontario
Australian agent: Thomas Nelson (Australia) Ltd,
                     597 Little Collins Street,
                     Melbourne, Australia.
New Zealand agent: Hodder & Stoughton Limited,
                     52 Cook Street,
                     Auckland C.1, New Zealand.
South African agent: Thomas Nelson & Sons
                     (South Africa) (Pty) Ltd,
                     Lewis and Marks Building,
                     65 President Street,
                     Johannesburg, South Africa.
East African agent: Thomas Nelson & Sons Ltd,
                     P.O. Box 25012,
                     Nairobi, Kenya.
West African agent: Thomas Nelson & Sons Ltd,
                     P.O. Box 336,
                     Apapa, Nigeria.
Israel agent: Steimatzky's Agency Ltd,
                     Citrus House,
                     P.O. Box 628,
                     Tel-Aviv, Israel.

Printed in Great Britain by
Hazell Watson & Viney Ltd
Aylesbury, Bucks

ONE

As soon as I came through the door I could see that they all had made it, every member of the Forty-two Club, and I was relieved and pleased. I told Anne so, but all she did was squeeze my arm and look around and I knew she was feeling a little ill at ease. After all, this was her first alumni reunion. I didn't want it to be her last, so I guided her to the group around the little bar I'd had set up in the conference room off the dining room. I ordered a pair of gin and tonics. It was a standard drink with Anne and me.

"Well, Prez," Jake Hardy said as he turned to us, saying it as if he were greatly surprised to see me, "glad you could make it." He showed his horsy white teeth in a big smile, and his eyes kept flickering to Anne. Being president of a group of seven men who graduated from Dorchester College in nineteen forty-two is hardly a signal honor, but Jake delighted in calling me "Prez," though nobody had ever called him that when he headed the group.

"Jake, I want you to meet Anne Whiting. Jake Hardy's a big man in San Benuto, Anne."

"You said it, Prez," he said, grinning at Anne, smoothing his black mustache with a forefinger, ice clinking in the nearly empty glass in his other hand. "You might say everybody depends upon me up there, Miss Whiting."

"At least all the drinking people do," I said, playing along.

"Just what do you do, Mr. Hardy?"

He chuckled, enjoying it. Maybe he was enjoying it too much because I said, "He's the municipal waterworks superintendent."

"Aw, you spoiled it." He was still smiling, but the lights had gone out in his eyes.

Anne said, "Why, that must be a very important job, Mr. Hardy," and I thought Bless you child, and was pleased to see the lights go on again.

I felt a hand like a ham slam into my back. I knew who it would be even before the hoarse voice said in my ear, "Phil, old boy," and Ernst Mollinauer's face bobbed into view. It was a flushed face. He stuck out his hand and I shook it while he said, "Sure glad to see you, fella." He nodded at Anne and I made the introductions. There was sweat on his forehead, but then there usually was. Ernst Mollinauer was a human dynamo despite his habits and his girth. A short, fat man, Ernst worked hard, lived hard. He enjoyed it.

"Ernst is one of the biggest foreign car dealers in Los Angeles,"

I told Anne. I could have told her he was probably the most prosperous man in the room. He'd inherited the place out on Sunset from his father and the recent surge in foreign car sales hadn't made him any poorer.

"Like those little cars?" he asked Anne.

"If you have a spare Renault Dauphine, I'll take it," she said.

"Listen to that girl," he said, pleased, turning to me. "Where've you been hiding her?"

"Not in a Renault Dauphine, I can tell you that."

"She'd look nice in one, though. Ever considered it, Phil?"

"Business isn't that good, Ernst."

"Hey, *hey!*" Another voice and another face. This one belonged to Poley McGowan, brother in misery, though he was a far more successful lawyer than I. But he'd had money and managed to buy into a big office. I had started from scratch. But I wasn't kicking. I was beholden only to me; Poley McGowan had three partners to contend with. "How are you, Phil?" He lit a cigarette in the end of his gold-ringed ebony holder.

"He's going to buy her a Dauphine," Ernst said.

"Really?" Poley's white eyebrows shot up. His grin flashed. "Can't say I blame him."

I made the introductions. "And I take the cases Baxter, Baxter, Stamper and McGowan won't handle."

"Don't you believe him, Miss Whiting," Poley said amiably. "He does all right. We'll get him into the firm one of these days." Talk calculated to make me feel good. Nice of him. But then, Poley was a nice guy. He'd been a standout in everything at Dorchester, and his white hair was his trademark. Blue-eyed, with an athlete's build—he'd been a fine Dorchester halfback—I knew Anne was impressed. But of course everybody was impressed by Poley McGowan.

Anne and I moved away from the bar and sat on folding chairs at one side of the room, and she said, "You know something?"

"What?"

"You're the youngest, best-looking man here."

"Well," I said, pleased as if I'd won my first case, "there's Herb Lincoln over there." I nodded my head in Herb's direction. "That's his wife beside him. Sophie is her name."

Anne glanced at them. "He's taller than you, but he's not better looking."

No one would call Dr. Herbert Lincoln good looking. He had a hawklike face, bushy eyebrows and the most intense eyes of any man I'd ever known. He was a neurologist and was much in demand in Los Angeles and San Francisco and points east. I had

8

been afraid he wouldn't be able to make this, the seventeenth annual get-together of the Forty-two Club.

"That's not what I meant, Anne. He's younger than I."

"My, he looks ten years older."

"He's really only a few months younger—he was the youngest man in the whole class. He'll be thirty-seven this fall." I told her what his profession was.

Anne nodded. "I thought it was something like that. I'll bet he's good at it, Phil."

"The best there is." No one would ever find me selling Dorchester grads short. I suppose I'm prejudiced.

She looked at me. I was sure it wasn't the gin and tonic that made her say, "And you're the best lawyer there is," and lean her head against my shoulder for a moment, giving my arm a squeeze with her hand. "Better than that Poley McGowan, I'll bet."

"Well," I conceded, "he did have money to start with. But he's one of the most successful."

"Not as successful as you'll be one of these days."

Everybody else was forgotten for the moment that I spent looking down into her eyes. Warm blue eyes filled with admiration for me. "I love you, Anne," I said.

She looked down at my hand and patted it. "I know my man." Then after a pause she said, "I guess you're stuck with me."

"I hope I never get unstuck, Anne."

At that moment Clifford Ellis moved away from the bar and came over to us, his drink in his hand, the usual sardonic grin on his face. He said, "Another year, another reunion. So help me I don't know why I come to the damn things."

"Sit down," I said, drawing a chair around for him. "If you don't enjoy it, I don't see why you come."

He sat. "Oh, I guess it's to see if anybody's lost more hair than I. Or just to compare the ageing process. I suppose I could write a book about it. A year by year account of the decline of seven young men, young no longer, filling their years with idiocy like this until that final day, that final graduation out of the whole thing." He drank his bourbon quickly. "I'm afraid it would never sell, though. People like tinsel, uplift, hope."

"This," I told Anne, "is Clifford Ellis. He——"

"You've got things wrong, Phil," Cliff said. "The other way around. Say the girl's name first, you fool. Didn't you learn anything in any of Miss Potter's classes on decorum at Dorchester? What is your name, my dear?"

"Anne Whiting. Was there really a class in decorum at Dorchester?"

Cliff laughed. "If there was, I wasn't in it."

"Clifford Ellis," I said. "He tries to live everything he writes. You'll notice, for example——"

"Ellis?" Anne said suddenly. "Why, I know your books." She turned to me. "You didn't tell me he was in your class."

I shrugged. "You didn't ask."

"Makes a difference, though, doesn't it, Anne?" Cliff said. "Now this whole affair suddenly becomes bearable. An interesting personage in our midst. Aren't you going to ask me for my autograph or where I get my ideas?"

"No, she isn't. And since Anne seems familiar with your work, she's probably wondering how you manage to turn out such junk and is just too polite to ask."

"You kill me," Cliff said, laughing. "To have one's creative children besmirched like that! You don't know what that does to the artistic side of me." Then he said in a phoney dramatic voice, "Just for that, Philip DeMoss, I challenge you to a duel at dawn tomorrow. My weapon will be book ends. Yours will be torts."

Anne laughed. "Are you always like this?"

"With a few more drinks I get even better. At least I think it's better. It depends upon the point of view."

"He hates breathing," I said. "Isn't it obvious?"

"I hate humanity. I hate my work. I hate living." He ran a hand over his close-cut bristling blond hair. Clifford Ellis was not unattractive, but there was a hardness about his eyes and mouth that matched his talk. "In fact," he went on, "to keep on living I need another drink right now." He rose. "If it weren't for the fact that I'm such a heel, I'd ask you two if you wanted one. But I won't."

"Well!" Anne said when he was gone.

"A little overwhelming, isn't he? He was the school's problem child. His grades were poor but his behaviour was worse. I don't think there's a rule he didn't break."

"These seven here tonight, they're not the only graduates of the Class of Forty-two, are they?"

"I should say not. I think there were over a hundred. Glenn Klock, he's the secretary this year, could tell us exactly. These seven happen to live in or near Los Angeles."

"You mentioned Glenn Klock. I don't think I've met him. Have I?"

"I don't think so." I looked around, spied him sitting with his wife in a corner of the room, pointed them out to her.

"He's so thin!" Anne cried out. Then she said more quietly, "I mean ascetic looking. And those glasses!"

"Glenn's the studious type. He always looks that way, hasn't changed much since school. He's quiet, reserved, and self-absorbed. He's an executive for North American Encyclopedia here in Los Angeles, and his only interests, as far as I know, are his wife and research work. He was brilliant in school."

"He looks as I'd expect a mad scientist to look. And did you say that is his wife?"

I nodded. "That's Lula."

"She's an exotic thing."

"Pretty nervous and flighty, from what Glenn says. I don't know them too well. She runs from one thing to another—ballet, dress designing, extension courses, dabbles in painting and poetry. Glenn has told it around, mostly for advice, I guess. Leaves her home too much, I think." I grinned at her. "I wouldn't leave you home. I'd be there every spare minute."

Anne was still thinking about the Klocks. "No children?"

"No children."

The program and the speeches were like the programs and speeches of other years. Poley McGowan made the principal address, as I'd asked him to, and he recounted the history of the class, made us all feel good, exemplary graduates as he said we were, cited some humorous happenings he remembered that we hadn't heard before. Then he said we were going on to be important men, that we were still young, that our best work was yet to be done. It was satisfying, and he was roundly applauded when he finished.

But somehow Clifford Ellis had spoiled it a little for me, his talk about the decline of seven young men filling their years with idiocy until—what did he say?—that last day, that final graduation. I looked around. Everybody seemed happy enough. Ellen McGowan happily congratulating her husband. The Klocks in agitated conversation. Ernst Mollinauer and his wife, Rose, grinning at each other, clapping. The Lincolns a little more staid than the others, but still enjoying it. Jake Hardy had a kind of glassy look. He hadn't touched much of his dinner. I guessed he had had a little too much to drink before dinner, which was par for his course. But he didn't look unhappy; He'd probably tell his San Benuto friends what a wonderful time he had. Maybe he *was* having a good time. Funny thing about Jake Hardy. Always the practical joker, he enjoyed playing deadpan until the joke came off, then he'd laugh louder than anyone else. But tonight he hadn't pulled a thing. Maybe he was growing up. In his early forties, perhaps it was time he did. Anyway, I wished he had sprung something. Anything.

Ellis himself didn't help. He was grinning, but it wasn't a healthy grin; there was a touch of evil in it, and I wondered what kind of man he really was beneath that loud, boastful exterior.

Later some of the others talked briefly, Herb Lincoln about his new work in neurology, particularly about some spare-time experiments in repairing brain damage of long standing, such as in epilepsy; Ernst Mollinauer cracked jokes about little cars and big people, and the jokes were pretty small and off-colour; with Anne Whiting by my side they didn't seem as funny this year.

Glenn Klock launched into a laborious and involved report of others in the class, marriages, professions, accomplishments, a rehash of what most of us had read in the Dorchester Alumni Bulletin, and halfway through I was forced to ask him to brief it down, and he cut it off shortly afterward, sitting down, embarrassed. Glenn had taken his job seriously, and I guess it never occurred to him that we didn't want him to be so thorough. But that was Glenn for you.

Jake Hardy managed to get off a couple raw jokes that fell flat, and then Cliff Ellis delivered his usual tirade against man, morals and mendacity. He was quite smug about it, and when it was over Anne whispered to me, "I don't think I like that man, Phil."

I said, "I don't think he likes himself, Anne."

Looking back on it, I can't recall that there was an odor of fear or hate or of death about any of it. They all seemed normal people safely embarked upon their worldly pursuits, growing stronger with the passing years. Certainly none of it seemed abnormal— *alien*—and nothing that was said or done that night gave any indication of the horrors to come. What could be more innocent, more innocuous than an annual gathering of congenial people, persons held together by the slender thread of their college affiliations? Yet it was in this relationship that the strange pattern of death was set, the dreadful future foretold, if one had only been able to see it.

It was late when the final drinks were drunk, the appropriate toasts made. I was tired and happy. Anne had been wonderful, I had been congratulated about her by everyone, and I wanted to retire from it while I was still ahead. I remembered a couple annual meetings where bitter words had ruined the evening at the end, and I didn't want this to happen, so I moved things along as fast as I could without rushing.

But it was Poley McGowan who approached us just before I was to settle up with the hotel.

"Phil," he said, "there's something I want to talk to you about." He was almost grave.

"Shoot, Poley. I was just about to pay the bill."

He glanced around. "Not here, Phil."

12

"There are lots of rooms," I said, glancing at Anne and wondering if I could leave her for a few minutes. "We could——"

"It's something important, Phil, and I don't mind at all if Anne listens in. Look, why don't you two come out to my place right now?"

"Well." Anne's face was indifferent. It said do what you want, Phil. In turning back to Poley, I saw Ellen McGowan's face smiling at us from across the room. "It's pretty late, Poley, and it's a long drive."

"Only thirty-five minutes. Come on. I don't think you'll regret it."

I said all right, but I was reluctant about it, even though he'd made me curious.

Poley's house was perfect for Poley. It was like him: large, big-boned, handsome and impressive. Off from Multiflora Drive in Bel Air, a crushed gravel drive wound through shrubbery and trees to the parking area before the house. The driveway was illuminated as brightly as any city street, yet it didn't seem garish or overdone. The house itself was made of stone, massive but not forbidding, and there was much glass. The front door was the only real door in the place; all others were sliding panels such as Japanese homes have. I always had the feeling when I entered the McGowan house that I ought to take off my shoes.

Even the floor was stone, but it was not cold stone, for it was radiantly heated. Poley enjoyed telling how he captured the day's heat for night, the night's coolness for day, air silently rushing beneath the floors twenty-four hours a day. Carpeting was inlaid, deep pile, and the first time I stepped on it I nearly fell flat on my face and Poley laughed.

The south part of the house was all glass, looking out to a grand view of Westwood and Mar Vista, to say nothing of the magnificent landscaping, the little teahouse, the not so little swimming pool and a stream where water trickled incessantly. Everything was modern, the big fireplace you could almost walk into, the electric kitchen, the dining area where Poley controlled lights, music and temperature with buttons beneath a heavy polished table. And everywhere there were plants: they were Ellen's department. It was hard to tell sometimes whether you were inside or out, the place had been designed so well.

"I'm glad you decided to come," Ellen McGowan said, leading us into the living room where a cheery fire blazed away in the fireplace. "Poley did so want you to."

A moment later her husband come out with gin and tonics. Poley said, "I know you're bushed, but I may not get a chance to talk to you like this again for a long time."

13

He reached into a box, brought out a cigarette, inserted it into his holder and lit it, his face serious. His eyes flicked to Ellen and he smiled. "You have quite a champion in Ellen, Phil. She can't understand why the firm doesn't take you in. She says it would be so much the stronger for it. And I think she's right."

Ellen McGowan smiled too. She was a year or two younger than Poley, a fine woman with warm dark eyes, elegance; but her elegance was not a chilling thing. She was a head shorter than her husband, dark-haired, and she had a way of moving that was easy and overwhelmingly feminine. She was also very intelligent, as I had learned on other visits.

She said now, "It's not my idea, Phil. Poley always asks me what do I think of this or that person, and when he was talking about it, why it seemed the best idea in the world."

"How about it, Phil?"

I hadn't ever considered it and I said so. "That's something I'd have to really think about, Poley. I don't even know if I'm cut out for that kind of stuff."

"I know we're specialized, but I don't think you'd ever regret it. Our workload is becoming so large it's beginning to get us down, and we don't want to buckle under. And you just can't take in somebody green. You can't take that chance. It's got to be somebody we know, somebody who's proved out." His eyes came up and they locked with mine. "It would mean your name on the door."

"Baxter, Baxter, Stamper, McGowan and DeMoss," I said. "Quite a mouthful. Mine is the only name on my door."

"I know that, Phil."

"Oh, I know what you mean, Poley, the prestige and all. I'm not denying that. But maybe I have to grow up to it. Maybe I'm not ready yet."

"You're ready, Phil. You don't know it, but I've been watching you. I should have talked to you before this."

"It's a tempting offer."

"Think about it."

"All right."

Then we were all talking at once, the tension had been broken, and it was good and I enjoyed being there and I know Anne did too. It was as if we'd been close friends for years. The four of us.

And then it was over and the McGowans were walking us to the car, Poley was shaking my hand and his wife was chatting with Anne. The whole night had taken on a good feeling and I was happy.

"I like them," Anne said, snuggling close to me as we drove down Multiflora Drive. "They're real people, lucky people."

14

"They have three children. Did you know that?"

"Ellen said they have a little playhouse for them out behind the teahouse. Patricia, Terry and—who's the youngest?"

"Clarence. He's a little imp."

Anne sighed. "They are lucky, a home like that, children."

"Poley was lucky to find a girl like Ellen," I said. I pulled the car over to the curb and took Anne in my arms. "And I want to tell you I feel lucky to have found you, darling."

When she got her breath, she said, "I was thinking the same thing." Then she laughed. "I don't mean that the way it sounded. I mean——"

I kissed her again. I knew what she meant.

As we drove on I began to think maybe Poley wasn't the only lucky one. Philip DeMoss seemed to be pretty lucky too.

And as it was, I was luckier than Poley.

A week later I was still alive and Poley was dead.

TWO

As president of the alumni group it fell to me to extend condolences to Mrs. McGowan, as well as to inform others of the group who might not know of Poley's death. Everywhere I was met with disbelief at first, then shock, and at such moments I found it difficult to believe that I was imparting such news. Everyone commented on Poley's cheerfulness at the dinner, his optimism, his position, wealth and future. They all said he was the last man in the world they thought would commit suicide.

I thought of his house, the beautifully landscaped yard and swimming pool, his wonderful wife and three children. I thought of his practice, his hopes for the future, his offer to me.

It just wasn't Poley, that's all. It couldn't have been. I told myself that over and over. But there was no denying the body fished out of the water at Ocean Park Pier. Mrs. McGowan identified it. What made matters worse, Poley had been seen walking into the ocean with his clothes on.

The newspapers quoted a man, one of several who were members of what was called the Spit and Argue Club and who sat almost every day at the ocean's side to discuss everything under the sun.

"It was like this picture with Fredric March," Harvey Sellington told newsmen. "This guy just walked into the water like he wanted to die. Didn't hesitate at all. We all watched him, and

15

when the water got up to his middle and the waves were coming in, we all started yelling. But he never heard us, I guess. Anyway, he never turned around or anything. He just kept going till he was gone."

Anne was terribly upset. "Why, Phil? Why?"

"I don't know," I told her on the phone.

"He was such a—a confident man. So sure of himself. And he had such a wonderful family, those three children. It must be a terrible time for his wife."

"I'm sure it is. I've got to go see her."

"If there's anything I can do, Phil . . ."

"Sure, Anne. I'll let you know."

The parking area in front of the McGowan house was filled with cars and I wondered vaguely who was there, but knowing of course there would have to be people there, relatives, friends, associates, and people whose business death was. I didn't expect to see anyone I knew, so I was surprised to see Sophie Lincoln. She rose from among several women seated at one end of the living room and came toward me.

"Herb was wondering if you were coming," she said. Sophie was almost as tall as her husband, which was tall indeed since he towered six feet two, but she was self-conscious about her height and walked with her shoulders hunched slightly forward, bent a little. Usually highly animated and whimsically natured, in contrast to Dr. Lincoln's cold, professional manner, now she was grave. Her face was almost stern, her manner was almost admonishing, as if she thought it would have been better if I had not come.

"He's with her now," she said. "She's taking it pretty hard."

"I don't doubt it. Poley was her whole life."

"If you've come to see her, I wish you wouldn't, Phil. I know how I would feel."

"I've got to. Poley and I were pretty close and she'd never forgive me."

She shrugged. "Herb thought you'd feel that way," she said, turning away to go toward the group she'd left.

I couldn't see why how I felt should make a great deal of difference to the Lincolns, but I didn't want to alienate anyone so I paused for a moment to consider it. Then I decided that I had as much right to be there as they did, and it might be that Ellen really wanted to see me and that I might be of real help. On the other hand, if I found my presence was painful to her, I could be brief.

Ellen McGowan and Herb Lincoln were in the rain room, which had been one of Poley's brainstorms, a room filled with tropical plants and a slanting glass roof upon which rain fell at the push of a button, if rain were not falling naturally. I had

16

found it restful and soothing on occasion; but it could be exciting too, particularly when Poley would initiate tape-recorded sound effects of thunder and wind. Now I saw Ellen and Herb sitting together in two of several reclining chairs, and they saw me at once. It was not raining—naturally or unnaturally—and I felt glad that it was not.

Herb rose at once. His manner was neither friendly nor unfriendly; he looked to Ellen for her reaction and so did I.

"Phil," she said. Her eyes were red-rimmed, her face waxy white. She tried to smile, but was not successful with it. "Come in." She reached out a trembling hand and I went over and took it. It was cold. "Sit down."

I drew up another chair. "You don't know how sorry I am, Ellen." I darted a glance at Herb, but his eyes conveyed nothing. When he started to sit down again, she said to him, "Would you leave us for a while, Herb?" He looked at her uncertainly for a moment, said, "Of course, Ellen," and left the room quietly.

Then Ellen turned to me. Her eyes were no longer as bleak as they had been. There was a hint of hard curiosity in them. She said, "I want to ask you something, Phil," and reached for my hand again.

I took her hand and told her I'd try to answer her if I could. From the pressure of her hand I knew her question must be terribly important.

"Why did Poley do it?"

I was shocked. She expected me to answer that? I didn't know what to say. Surely she would know why better than I.

"I—I don't know, Ellen. I thought maybe you'd know. I know it was sudden and something I never expected——"

"He didn't come to see you?" Her eyes were brighter.

"Come to see me?"

"He didn't come? He didn't call?"

"No. I haven't seen him or heard from him since the annual meeting."

She seemed relieved and I didn't know why, then. She sank back in the chair and closed her eyes. "Poor Poley," she said. "Poor, poor Poley."

It was quiet and I didn't know what to say to her. Now I wished the rain were falling. That would have been a distraction, something soothing. Its absence now made the silence brittle, fragile, something painful to break.

But I had to say, "How did it happen?"

She shook her head without opening her eyes. "I don't know." Something about the way she said it, something in her manner made me wish she had looked at me as she said it.

17

"Poley wasn't the kind of a guy who'd go walk into the ocean, Ellen." Then after a pause I added, "I thought he was the luckiest, happiest man I knew."

Instead of the reaction I expected, Ellen McGowan broke out in a cry she must have been holding back. Her hands went to her face, she leaned forward in the chair and became a sobbing woman. I moved from my chair to put my arms about her, but it was as if I weren't there.

Just then a woman I did not know came through the door, followed by Herb Lincoln, who motioned for me to join him. The woman, it turned out, was a nurse Herb had provided. At the door Herb did not move away, but when the door closed behind me he studied me with those black eyes of his and I half expected him to say, "Why did you do it, Phil?" But he didn't.

He said instead, "Did she ask you if he came to see you?"

Surprised, I said, "Yes, she did. Did she ask you, too?"

Herb nodded. "Did it seem to you she thought it a very important question?" His eyes flickered a little. "And did the question seem strange to you?"

"Yes, it did, Herb."

He sighed, ran three fingers of his right hand across his forehead. I'd seen him do that many times, mostly when he was in serious thought or trouble or trying to remember something. "There is something odd about all this, Phil, something more than a man just walking into the ocean. I've worked with people in times of stress. I have had to go out and tell a man's wife there isn't any hope for her husband, and I've been met with many different reactions, but there is something peculiar about Ellen McGowan's." It was almost as if he were talking to himself. His eyes were distant, reminiscent, and I could almost see in them the situations he described being repeated over and over. "And," he went on, "it isn't so much what she said as the way she said it."

The shock of having said something that sent her into grief was slowly passing and now I began to sense what Herb meant. Why had it seemed so important to Ellen whether or not Poley had been to see me? Why had her eyes been so bright and curious? Furthermore, what difference would it have made? What if he *had* visited us? What comfort could there be in the knowledge that he had?

But wait, the first thing she had asked was, "Why did Poley do it?" And she had sent Herb away so she could ask me. Now why had she done that? And why the devil should she ask it? She was so tense, her hand was so tight in mine when she did, that when I said I didn't know why, she seemed actually cheered that I

18

didn't know. And then she seemed relieved that Poley hadn't come to see me. That wasn't right.

Herb wasn't alone in dealing with people. I had seen them, all types and sizes, in my years in the legal profession. Frustrated, angry, depressed, vindictive people, people with grudges, with sad hearts, with axes to grind. No. Herb wasn't alone in his experiences with people. I'd had my share.

But he was also right. There *was* something strange in Ellen McGowan's reaction.

He said, "It's as if she holds herself to blame."

I hadn't been struck exactly that way. With me it was more that Ellen McGowan seemed to be holding something back, and I told Herb so. He shrugged and we commenced walking down the hallway.

One of the doors ahead of us slid open and Clarence McGowan's head appeared in the opening. He was a towheaded youngster with the large, luminous eyes of his mother. When he saw us his eyes brightened with lively interest. The youngest of the McGowan clan, I'd guess he was about eight years old.

"Hullo," he said, smiling.

We said hello, were abreast of him, and I looked into the room he'd come out of. A woman was seated with the two other McGowan children, Patricia, the oldest, about eleven, and Terry, who was in between. I didn't know the woman, but she had Ellen's features and I guessed she was her sister.

"Come back, Clarence," the woman said from the long divan where she had been reading to them.

I had seen Clarence before and I saw that he recognized me but probably didn't know my name, so I said, "I'm Philip DeMoss."

"My name is Clarence. Won't you come in? Aunt Betty's reading us a story." He pushed the door open to admit us. Herb and I stood there undecided.

The woman rose from the divan and when she did the older boy, who had been leaning against her shoulder and fallen asleep, slumped to the divan seat, stirred a little and then was quiet. The girl, Patricia, glanced at him and then got up too.

"I'm Betty Lathrop," Aunt Betty said, advancing. Patricia hovered in her wake.

"It's Phil," Clarence said, as if that explained everything.

I patted his head. "Philip DeMoss. This is Dr. Lincoln."

"How do you do. I met Dr. Lincoln earlier." She was, I guessed, a little older than Ellen, but there was much the sameness about the eyes, the lips and the way she carried herself.

"We didn't mean to intrude. Hello, Patricia."

"Hello, Mr. DeMoss." Patricia's voice was toneless, her face

19

was pale. She didn't want to look at me. But then Ellen hadn't either.

"You were a friend of Poley's. A lawyer friend."

I said I was. She said, "Ellen has mentioned your name." For a moment there was an awkwardness where there shouldn't have been, and I think it was caused by Patricia's reluctance to come forward. Then awkwardness was dispelled by a low moaning from the divan and we all turned to Terry.

The boy was whimpering, moving his lips, his hands.

"No," he said in a low voice. "No, Daddy. Please."

We started for him, Herb and I, with Betty behind us, Patricia already at his side, staring at him with wide eyes.

Terry went on, "Don't come near me, Daddy. No. *No!*" Then he screamed and cried, "I hate you, I hate you!" His cry was high and quavering and it filled more than the room, and I could feel it go out in the hall and reach the room Ellen was in, and I shuddered.

Herb went over, shook the boy. Terry woke, terror in his eyes, looking beyond us, seeking the object of his terror in corners of the room. Betty Lathrop was at his side on the divan in an instant and he buried his face in her shoulder, sobbing uncontrollably.

Ellen McGowan came rushing through the door and into the room, taking Terry from Betty, stroking his head and saying, "It's all right, Terry, it's all right," tears falling on his neck. Patricia stood to one side. I thought from the look of her she would faint any moment. Clarence was clinging to Aunt Betty, who was staring at Ellen and Terry.

Then others rushed into the room.

Later, I asked Herb, "What do you make of it?"

He shrugged. "It was a dream."

"A dream can have significance. Ask any psychoanalyst."

"Do you think this one has?"

"I don't know, Herb. Do you?"

"I don't know, either. I know the brain as an architect knows his building, as a radioman knows his circuits. I also know it is possible to hide things in it. Sometimes they come out in an epileptic seizure. Or in a dream."

"You think that's what has happened here?"

"Maybe. I said I really don't know. I'm afraid we'll never know."

We were standing just outside the house and people kept going in and coming out. Glenn Klock had come and gone and Ernst Mollinauer was still inside paying his respects. I knew I had seen Frank and Sam Baxter, two of Poley's partners. Other than

20

that I knew none of the people. As one, Herb and I started on the path around the house to the swimming pool, saying nothing, seeing the visitors inside through the glass, seeing too the calm of the pool, the neatness of the grass. Perhaps we should have left, but we were held there by the sorrow in the house and the strangeness, too.

"A man," Herb said, "can show a different face at home. It might be that we didn't know Poley McGowan at all."

I was going to say that I didn't think that could be true in Poley's case, when we rounded the pool and came upon the tea-house where an old man sat eyeing us, grinning. He had a half-empty bottle of wine on the table before him.

"Come in, gentlemen, come in," he said. It was obvious he was drunk and that this was not his first bottle of the day. "Come in and join a rat in a drink."

He was Davenport, Poley's gardener and handyman, I remembered now, and I put a hand on Herb's arm because I sensed that Herb thought this was an outrage, this man sitting here drunk. I told him who he was.

"This is no place for you," Herb said. "You are a disgrace to Mrs. McGowan in your condidtion. You'd better get out of here before somebody else sees you."

Davenport squinted at us. "I suppose," he said thickly, "you're wondering why Mr. McGowan's dead."

"We know why he's dead," I said. "Now why don't you do as Dr. Lincoln says. If you must drink, you'd better do it at home."

"Oh, no, you don't know why he's dead. Not really, you don't. So you're a doctor, eh? Well, you wouldn't know either. *I* know why he's dead."

"Suppose," Herb said, "you tell us why you think he's dead."

"Because I killed him," Davenport said. He was a man in his early sixties, white-haired, thin and wrinkled. He leered across the table at us.

"What makes you think you killed him?" I asked.

"Because I wasn't nice to him, that's why," he said, staring in drunken fascination at the ground before our feet. "I wasn't nice to him at all." His face wrinkled up, his eyes closed and his mouth drew down. "He was the best friend I ever had," he said between compressed lips, "and I let him down. I wasn't nice to him after—after he changed." His head dropped to the table and the wine bottle went scooting over the edge to the bricks below and broke. Davenport sobbed.

We tried to get him to tell us what he meant, but all we could get out of him was that some sort of personality change had occurred, and while I knew Herb was thinking in terms of psychiatric things, my mind was recalling stories of possession and the inhabitation of one being by another.

A little later we both dismissed the maunderings of a drunken man as of no value.

We couldn't have been more wrong.

THREE

The next day I tried putting it all out of my mind and concentrating on business, and it worked—for an hour. I saw people, I made several appointments, and I even managed to make a few phone calls, all my usual office routine, before it all filtered past the barriers I had erected against it and Miss Selma Livingston, my secretary, came into my office to tell me she had been trying to get me on the intercom. I suppose I must have looked pretty stupid sitting there behind my desk staring at nothing across the room and oblivious to such a vital link as the communications system.

It was Anne on the phone and I made a date for lunch with her. She asked me if anything was wrong I sounded odd, and I told her I'd tell her all about it when I saw her. Then I knuckled down the rest of the morning and cancelled the remainder of the day, which was neither wise nor profitable but was what I felt I had to do. There were threads that had to be unravelled.

"I'm worried about you, Phil," Anne said when we had ordered our lunch at Filiponi's. "You didn't sound right, you don't look yourself. You shouldn't let a thing like this get you down. It *is* Poley's death, isn't it?"

"Yes, but it's not that I'm morbid about it. It's just that there are a lot of things that don't make sense." I told her about Ellen, her questions, Terry McGowan's dream, Herb's ideas, Davenport's drunkenness and self-debasement. "I think I owe it to Poley to try to get some answers."

"Don't tell me you don't think he walked into that water!"

"I don't know. Oh, I guess he did. But there's more to it than that. We don't know why, for example."

"But Phil, people do things like that every day and relatives and—friends like you—are left to wonder why." Seeing the wry look on my face, she went on, "Oh, I know what you mean, all right. There are so many—what do you lawyers say?—extenuating circumstances." She flashed me a sympathetic smile and laid her hand over mine. "I'm with you, Phil. If you think there's

22

something funny going on, so do I. I know how you feel about Poley. But I want you to promise me something."

I said I would, what was it.

She said, "Just let me know what you find out."

No expense had been spared in the offices of Baxter, Baxter, Stamper and McGowan in Beverly Hills. There were rugs ankle-deep. There were good-looking girls, secretaries and receptionists that would put Selma Livingston to shame probably in all departments except that of the business of efficiently helping to run a law office. They were too distracting. But the wood on the walls was genuine. The brass ash trays were heavy. In fact, there was richness, affluence, wealth everywhere. But there was also an aloofness and coolness that alienated me. I have always operated on the assumption I was offering something to the public and I kept my office cheerful and friendly, and I'd instructed Selma to be cordial and helpful. This place said you'd better be brief (we're busy), you'd better have money (you'll need it), and you'd better make it worth our while (are you important enough?).

I'd seen it before, of course. Heretofore I had reserved my opinion because Poley had chosen to be a part of it. Now that he was no longer here, I could be candid with myself without fear of hurting him.

I had to wait a half hour to see Sam—pardon me, I mean Samuel—Baxter. Frank Baxter wasn't in town and Edwin Stamper, the other partner, conducted half his business at a Federal Savings and Loan down the street. Beverly Hills property presupposed someone like Edwin Stamper to handle it. Sam Baxter's secretary was ornate and young—ornate because she had been endowed by nature with an excess of all the good things, and young because she blushed when I couldn't keep my eyes off her. Perhaps innocent would be a better word. Or maybe even inexperienced. Anyway, she had difficulty typing a transcript. I wondered idly what talents she possessed (beside the obvious ones) that kept her there. For all I could see of her work, it could have been her first day. I ceased thinking about her though when she said Mr. Baxter will see you now.

Samuel Baxter was the senior partner. He was big in every way, heavy featured, lumbering and possessed of a pair of the shrewdest eyes I've ever seen. He did me the honor of getting up from behind his mammoth batwing desk and coming around to shake my hand, his smile a display of white teeth. He was dressed in a tailored pin-stripe suit and conservative tie. Very impressive.

"Glad to see you, Phil," he said heartily, pumping my hand.

23

"Come and sit down." He pulled a chair away from the wall. "Drink?"

"No thanks, Sam. But don't let me stop you."

"Oh, no, my boy. Too early for me." He went around and sat in his big reclining chair that reminded me more of a judge's chair than an attorney's. "Poley told me he'd offered you something." His cough was just right. "I don't know where his passing puts us."

"That's not what I came here to talk about, Sam."

"Tragic about Poley. It set us all back." He paused a moment as in mourning, then went on guardedly, "What *did* you come to talk about, Phil?"

"Poley."

"Poley?" Sam's sagebrush eyebrows went up a notch and I knew I had caught him by surprise. Not that it meant anything. The eyebrows went down again. "What about Poley?" Now there was suspicion in his eyes.

I set him at ease. "Nothing, really. I just wondered about his last days here, that's all. He was a good friend. I'm just trying to figure out why he should have done what he did."

"We all do, Phil. He was happy. In fact, sometimes I thought he wasn't staid enough for us. Not enough reserve, if you follow me. He was the last person—but I suppose you think so too."

"Yes." I brought out my pipe and Sam said he had some special tobacco he had mixed and would I try it. I did. It wasn't bad. "What I really want to know, Sam, is: Did Poley exhibit any symptoms—anything at all that might throw some light on his death?"

He was troubled. "I'm afraid I can't answer that, Phil."

"You can't answer it? What do you mean?"

"Well, I didn't see him for about a week before it happened."

"Oh. You were away. Out of the office, I suppose. Well, was Frank here? Or Ed?"

Sam seemed embarrassed. "No, Phil, I wasn't away. It's not that at all."

"Well, what is it then?"

He clapped both palms to his forehead, something I'd never seen Sam Baxter do before. Then he said, blowing out his breath, "Phil, Poley wasn't in the office for a week."

"Wasn't in the office?" That floored me. "Where the devil was he then?"

"I don't know why I shouldn't tell you, Phil. He was at home. As far as I know he didn't leave the house for the whole week."

I must have stared at him because he said, "Oh, come now,

Phil, what does that prove? He said he wasn't feeling good, so we thought it best he stay home, just as he suggested."

"He suggested it?"

"Yes. The office boy took the mail out to him each day. He sent back dictation for Elizabeth to transcribe. I really don't think the office suffered much and I don't think he could have been very ill, judging from the amount of work he turned out. He has—had—as good a law library at home as we have here."

"You didn't think it was strange that he should work at home?"

"Well, not exactly. As a matter of fact, I admired him for it. I've thought about doing that very thing, but I've never had the fortitude." He smiled again. "Besides, Ruth wouldn't stand for it. Always insists I get in the way, interrupt her routine if I'm home off schedule."

That changed things. Except for what Davenport had hinted at, I had thought Poley had behaved normally the last week of his life. This was something else. Still, he couldn't have been home *all* the time because Ellen had asked me if Poley had come to see me, and she'd asked Herb, too. Why hadn't she mentioned that Poley'd been home all week? But of course she wasn't thinking straight. Now I began to wonder what he'd been like at home, in just what way he had changed—if he had changed—and I confess I began to entertain notions about possession again. But I knew I couldn't ask Ellen. At least not right now.

But I might ask Davenport.

Sam was saying, "I understand Poley called Elizabeth several times. Changes in things he dictated, and so on. She's in his office now, I think. If it will give you any peace of mind, perhaps you ought to talk to her."

I said I would like to and Sam checked on his intercom and found that Elizabeth Potter was indeed in Poley's office. I walked what seemed like a city block down a carpeted corridor to the office Sam referred me to and found Elizabeth there. She was in Poley's outer office and she rose when I entered.

"You're Mr. DeMoss," she said.

"Yes." Although I had visited Poley on several occasions, this office was different from the last one he had. Elizabeth was different too. For the life of me I couldn't recall Poley's other secretary's name, the one I had seen before. But Elizabeth was all woman. I decided it was a company rule.

"Mr. McGowan was a friend of mine," I told her. "I think his suicide was most unlike him and I was wondering if you detected anything unusual in his behavior during the last week, other than the fact that he spent it at home."

We sat down and Elizabeth gave every evidence of trying to think of what I had asked her. Her eyes were beautiful—large and brown and flecked with blue—and honest. Her lips were full and red. Her hands were fine-boned.

"I don't know that there was anything unusual," she said in a well-modulated voice. "Somebody said maybe he had small-pox or something." She reddened a little. "Just office talk. Other than that, I really don't know, Mr. DeMoss."

"You don't know the reason he stayed home?"

"Oh, he was ill."

"You talked to him on the phone?"

"Certainly, I did. There were a couple things in letters I didn't understand—he had a bad habit of slurring things once in a while. But he said I should call him up if I didn't understand. So I did."

"And he sounded normal?"

"Well, I wouldn't say normal. What I mean is he seemed—well, he seemed bothered by something."

"Bothered? Bothered by what?"

"I don't know."

"I see. Would you say he seemed depressed?"

"Oh, part of the time he was. He sounded more tired, though. Worried, too. I think it's pretty hard to get a mood over the phone. Don't you think so?"

"I suppose so." But I really didn't think so.

"But I never thought he'd do what he did."

"When was the last time you talked to him?"

"The Friday before he did it—I mean the Friday before he died."

"A couple days before he walked into the ocean. How'd he seem that Friday?"

"He seemed good. I mean, he seemed better than usual. He said he was coming back to the office Monday morning." Her eyes left mine and wandered to her hands. "He even joked about my wearing a bright red sweater I have. He said he wanted to see me in it again. He said it cheered the whole office."

I could see how it would. "But he didn't show up on Monday," I said, wanting to get away from the bright red sweater.

"No, he didn't. I got the dictation and tried to call out to his house, but nobody answered. I didn't know until the next day what happened to him."

I drove around Los Angeles trying to get myself to forget the whole thing. I had a living to make, good work that I enjoyed. Of course this was nothing but an afternoon out of my life devoted to Poley, but I knew if I let it, it could become an obsession, attempting to reconstruct Poley's last days. And what would be the point? If it was simply a case of a man going off the deep end and ending up in the ocean, then mine was simply a morbid interest. If it was more than that, though, it would be worth while pursuing.

Had Ellen driven Poley to suicide? If so, what was that to me? All I could do was hate her for it, except that I don't think I could do that unless she had been really unscrupulous, and there wasn't an unscrupulous bone in her body, as far as I knew. No, there was more to it than that. I was sure Herb felt the same way. But so help me I couldn't put my finger on what was wrong, even though an inner sense kept telling me there was.

I wanted to talk to somebody else, somebody conservative and studious and steady, so I parked the car and made a call to Glenn Klock. As a researcher, he was used to weighing facts soberly without letting too much of humanity get between him and his problem. But he was out of the office. I could have driven up to San Benuto to see Clifford Ellis and probably interrupt him in the middle of another one of his incisive novels and be cursed roundly for it, but I didn't want to go that far. Of course Jake Hardy was in San Benuto and I could have seen him, but I didn't think Jake would be much help. He was friendly and alive, but he seemed more of a surface thinker. We'd probably end up getting tight together and recounting glorious Dorchester days. Or swapping stories.

In the car again I found myself on Sunset near Ernst Mollinauer's plush foreign-car salesroom. I hadn't thought of Ernst, but now that I did I knew he would be good to talk to. He might have inherited his business, but he was wise, shrewd and aware of the ways of the world behind that hail-fellow-well-met exterior he presented to everyone.

I parked the car and went in. Instantly a friendly-looking young man in a conservative business suit detached himself from a group of other friendly-looking young men in conservative business suits and came toward me with a big smile. But I waved him away because I saw Ernst talking to another man at the side of a small convertible. The other man, I saw to my surprise was Cliff Ellis.

"Hiya," Ernst said in his most disarming way, lifting his elbow from a shiny fender and offering his big ham of a hand.

"Well, well," Cliff said, not moving from his stance at the side of the car, "he's come after that Dauphine for that girl of his. Ernst, I don't see how you do it."

Ernst laughed as we shook hands. "I wish I handled them.

27

That's one car I'm missing. Good seller, too." He patted the convertible Cliff was leaning against. "Ever consider a Rapier, Phil? This is a Sunbeam Rapier. Dual carburetors and you can attain a top speed of eighty-three miles per hour."

"Phil's not the fast type," Cliff said. "But I think maybe Anne is. Am I right, Phil?"

"Zero to sixty miles an hour in nineteen seconds," Ernst said. "Want to try it?"

"Cut it out. I don't have the money or the inclination. I still drive an old Chevvy."

"You should be driving one of those other big chromy Detroit monstrosities complete with all its ornate sexual symbols," Cliff said.

"Your talk cheers me," Ernst said, "but you've got Phil all wrong." He stepped back as if to study me. "I see before me a man who ought to be in a custom-built Devin Porsche."

"A screaming bomb," Cliff said. "I don't see Phil in it at all. Too conscientious, too devoted to causes. In short, just too nice a guy, aren't you, Phil?"

"Opposites attract," I said. "Maybe that's why I still like you, Cliff."

"No, Mr. DeMoss. The only reason you tolerate me is our affiliation with Dorchester College. An umbilical cord we never seem to be able to sever."

"Nasty talk for a nice afternoon," Ernst said, bringing out a handkerchief and wiping away the ever-present sweat from his forehead. "I suggest a truce. I won't try to sell anything, and, Cliff, you can stow the sarcasm." He smiled again. "Nice to have you drop in, Phil. I mean it."

Cliff rendered his sardonic smile. "I guess I do, too, if I'm to be under oath."

"We were just talking about Poley when you came in," Ernst said, shaking his head. "I hate to see a thing like that happen."

I had intended to talk to Ernst about it fully, but I said only, "I don't think anything's ever shocked me as much."

"He was a good guy," Cliff said grudgingly. "One of the best." He shrugged. "Who knows, though? Maybe he's better off."

Ernst said, "You can't mean that, Cliff. He had everything to live for. Good business, wife, children, a home."

"You're in love with life, Ernst. All you need to do is look at you and you can tell that."

"I suppose you're not," I said.

"I endure it," he said soberly. "All its slings and arrows."

"You don't enjoy it?" Ernst asked.

28

"The only joy I get is striking back once in a while. For the most part it's for the birds."

"You've never been in love," Ernst said.

"Love? I'm always in love."

I said, "I don't think you know what the word means."

"Oh, yes, I do, Phil. Know something? I've been hurt. Does that help?" He smiled wryly. "Maybe that explains a few things. You understand I don't do this chest-baring act for everybody."

Ernst nodded. "If you walked into the ocean, Cliff, I'd understand it. It would be a protest. Right? But not Poley. He had nothing to protest."

Cliff ran a hand over his bristling hair. "I guess he didn't. I know people. At least I think I know people. Writers are supposed to be able to take them apart like a watch. But I had Poley all wrong."

"Did he call either of you last week?" I asked. "Or did he come to see you?"

They looked at me blankly. Then Cliff said, "He never called me. Ever. At least not that I remember. And I didn't see him. Never left San Benuto the whole week."

Ernst was frowning. "Funny about that. First time I've thought about it." He brightened. "Poley was going to buy a car. Another car. Wanted a small one for Ellen. We were talking about a Borgward Isabella or a Volvo. Both are fast. But he was inclined to think along the lines of a Fiat."

"When was this?" I asked.

"More than a week ago. Then last week I called Poley up at his office and he wasn't there and they wouldn't tell me where he was. So I called out at the house. It was Wednesday, I think."

Cliff was interested. "You talk to him, Ernst?"

"Sure." He ran the handkerchief across his forehead again. "That's the funny part. He didn't sound like Poley at all."

"What did he sound like?" I prodded.

"Oh, I don't know. He said he couldn't talk about it right then. I asked him when he thought he could talk about it, but he said he didn't know. He sounded down in the mouth and so I asked him if he was feeling O.K. He said sure he was, but he was just busy. He said he'd drop around when it was all over."

"When it was all over?" This was something new.

"Yeah. He sounded so beat I didn't want to press him by asking him what he meant. I just said O.K., any time, Poley, and decided to let him take his own sweet time."

Cliff said, "He was having some kind of trouble. You know, Jake Hardy called me up to talk about Poley and he said he didn't think Poley was himself the night of the dinner. Maybe he was right."

"Oh, there was nothing wrong then, Cliff," Ernst said. "I could have sworn there wasn't."

I said, "I didn't think there was either."

Cliff nodded. "Maybe so. My guess is he had some kind of nervous breakdown or something. He had to have *something*. Otherwise why should he go walk into the ocean?"

Ernst said, "Yeah," and looked thoughtfully out the salesroom window. "It could have happened to any of us. You never know about things like that. A guy is O.K. one day, the next day—poof!"

We got on more cheerful subjects and talked for a while, then I got in the car and went out to the McGowan house. I didn't go in. I didn't want to say anything to Ellen yet, but I hoped I'd find a sober Davenport. I did. He was trimming a hedge. It was a long way from the house and I was glad it was.

He nodded as I came up. "Mr. DeMoss," he said.

"Davenport," I said. He stopped the clippers and looked at me.

He said, "Sorry about what I did the other day. I was feeling bad. I'm over it now."

I didn't think he'd remember it. "It was the shock."

"Yeah. It was plenty bad."

I got out my pipe, filled it while I tossed questions around in my head. When I had the right one, I said, "Look, Davenport, did Poley act peculiar during the week he was here at the house?"

I never saw such a change in a man. His face drained of color, his hands shook and the whites of his eyes became more prominent. He was a man afraid and he ran a tongue along his lips as he said, "Please, Mr. DeMoss, you ain't going to ask me nothing about that, are you?"

"Sure. Why not?"

He clamped his mouth shut and swallowed. Hard. "I wish you wouldn't. I don't want to talk about it."

"Why, Davenport?"

"I can't, Mr. DeMoss. I just can't. Don't ask me."

"Was it something horrible? You act as if it were."

He swallowed again, started the clippers. They made a lot of noise. He turned his back on me.

I stepped around him, faced him. "Look here, Davenport, if there was something peculiar—"

He stopped the clippers, dropped them and backed away. "I can't talk. I told you that. Go away. I told Mrs. McGowan I wouldn't tell anybody, not even you. Now go!" When he saw I wasn't going to leave, his face betrayed his even more frightened state and he turned his back on me and ran toward the house, an old, frail man who shouldn't have run as fast as he did.

As it was it didn't matter, really.

Ernst Mollinauer was dead a week later and I forgot about Davenport then.

FOUR

It happened on a Saturday night when Anne and I had gone out on the town, when we were talking about the things people in love talk about, people seriously in love, such as when the big day ought to be, whether it ought to be a big wedding or not. Anne's parents were moderately well-to-do Pasadena people—her father owned a jewelry store where Anne worked when she was needed —and while Anne said she'd be willing to bow to my demands for a small church affair, she wasn't sure her mother and father would stand still for it.

"As long as you're marrying me for my money," she said, "you might as well come around to thinking the way they do." She was kidding of course, but I liked her parents well enough to want to do what would please them. My folks, who lived in Van Nuys, had long ago given up and considered me a permanent bachelor. Anything I would decide to do along marital lines would be all right with them.

We talked of proper churches, of where we would live, what kind of house. We talked about children and what we would name them. Anne went on at great length about what she wanted in the house, and I went on at great length about what I wanted in my study.

"And there will be a study," I said with finality, "an impressive one. Maybe it will even have a fireplace."

"I don't care what it has," Anne said, "I'll invade it."

"I'll lock the door. A man has to have a place to escape to."

"I'll learn how to pick locks."

I sighed. "Well, maybe there oughtn't be a lock. I don't like barriers."

"That's more like it. A bearskin rug in front of the fireplace. I'll bring you coffee."

It went on like that as we moved from place to place. It was fun, talking about the future, and I knew it was going to be wonderful with Anne wherever it was spent. But eventually we exhausted the subject and returned to current things and things

31

just past, and Anne said she was glad I hadn't discovered anything earthshaking in Poley McGowan's death.

"Of course I wanted you to be satisfied," she said, "and I know you're not, really. But I think it's simply because you were too close to Poley."

"Maybe so." It had been several days since I'd been preoccupied with it.

"I think it's a plain case of overwork and nerves. He didn't go down to the office because his nerves were giving way and he didn't want to make a display of it."

I said, "Just the same, I can't get the picture of Davenport out of my mind. He was afraid, Anne."

"Who wouldn't be afraid of someone disintegrating as Poley must have? He probably didn't know what was wrong with him. Here was a man normally kind and attentive and soft-spoken. Suddenly he's an entirely different man. Davenport probably didn't understand it at all."

"But would Ellen tell him not to talk to anyone about it?"

"Of course, darling. She took a great pride in her husband. She wouldn't want people to know, that's all."

There was no answer. "I suppose you're right."

"Even the kids probably bore some of it. Being around somebody in the middle of a thing like that isn't the most pleasant thing in the world."

I was ready to agree with her.

Except that later that night I learned about Mollinauer.

I had taken Anne home, returned to my apartment in Glendale, and was making myself a nightcap when the phone rang. It was Herb Lincoln.

"Ernst Mollinauer's dead," he said.

"Dead?" I repeated foolishly. It still didn't register as reality. A dull statement of fact with no possible meaning for me.

"He jumped or was pushed from the bedroom window of his third-floor apartment a little while ago. I happened to be here at the hospital when they came back with him. He was dead on arrival."

"Herb," I said, the news travelling slowly from my ear to my brain where it set a panicky feeling going, "who would want to kill Ernst Mollinauer?"

"His wife maybe."

"Rose?" I couldn't believe it. "No, Herb. Not Rose. They were too close, too happy."

I could feel his shrug. "She was in the bedroom at the time."

"Did she say she did it?"

"The police think she might have. She was in the room Ernst

32

went tumbling from. They were both in pajamas. Looks as if they had a quarrel or something, police said. I thought I'd let you know. Not very pretty, is it?"

"Did they arrest her?"

"No. She's here now. Won't talk. Shock."

"Poor Rose."

"She told the police one thing, Phil."

"What's that?"

"She said Ernst jumped, she didn't push him. But then she really went into a reaction. I've been down to see her. She doesn't look good."

I let out my breath. "First Poley and now Ernst."

Herb said coldly, "I'll admit it's odd."

I had a sudden thought. "What about the kids?"

"What about them?"

"Kelly and Karen. They are little tots, not in school yet. They haven't been left in the apartment, have they?"

Pause. "I don't know, Phil. I'd better check on that."

I let him go, telling him to call me back, and he said he would. Then I sat down with my drink. If Ernst Mollinauer jumped from his bedroom window, what was so different between that and walking into the ocean? Both accomplished the same purpose.

And how unlike both Poley and Ernst! Two people whom you would least expect to do a thing like that. Two very successful men, both with families, assured incomes, friends and associates, community leaders. And within two weeks of each other. I shuddered and started to think about familiars, hexes, zombies and aliens again. The situation was too bizarre for commonplace explanation. Like psychiatry, for example. I didn't doubt for a moment that there was a connection between the deaths and something supernatural.

Another odd thought struck me. Both men were Dorchester grads of the Class of 1942. Probably the most successful, if you took money, position and family into consideration. And both as unlikely to do a thing like this as—well, as any of us.

My mind was in a whirl and I couldn't get off. I had to get another drink to make it slow down a little. It didn't help much. I debated calling Anne, but thought what would that accomplish but interrupt her sleep. I also considered calling some of the others in the class, but thought the better of that too. They'd learn about it soon enough in the papers this time.

A little later Herb called me. He was brisk and brief and seemed hurried. He said he learned the Mollinauer kids were with their grandmother in Pacoima, that they'd been there most of the week.

I said I thought that was peculiar, didn't he? He said he couldn't stop to chat and hung up.

I had another drink and finally got to sleep.

The next morning I awoke with alarm bells ringing in my head. It seemed clear to me in the light of day there had to be a connection between Poley's death and Mollinauer's, so I called up Selma to tell her I wouldn't be in the office right away, that in fact I might not be in all day, I didn't know, I'd call her. Next I got in touch with Anne and told her about Ernst, and she was horrified. Also, she didn't want me to do anything about it.

"Go to the police," she said. "Let them do the investigating, not you, Phil."

"The police already know about it. They're busy investigating it right now, and probably they've satisfied themselves about Poley McGowan. Besides, what could I tell them? They'd throw me out if I told them what I'm thinking."

"I know it's fantastic," she said, "but I feel as you do that this isn't just coincidence." Then after a pause, she said, "Be careful, Phil. Remember I love you. I wouldn't want anything like that to happen to you."

"I'm not jumping off any bridges or anything, darling."

"There's always a first time. It's usually the last."

I tried to make light of it, told her not to worry, I'd call her if and when I uncovered anything, and then broke off the connection. The phone rang almost at once. It was Glenn Klock.

"Phil," he said, "I just heard about Ernst on the radio while I was having breakfast. Is it all true?"

"I'm afraid it is, Glenn."

"Lula doesn't want me to leave the house. She says there's a conspiracy afoot to do away with the Forty-two Club man by man."

"I don't know about that, Glenn, but nobody's doing away with the members but the members themselves. It's not as if it's murder. Poley walked into the ocean and Ernst fell or jumped out a window."

"That business about Rose being in the room, Phil. She couldn't have done it."

I thought so too, but I said, "Why not?"

"Man, you're mad. Rose couldn't do a thing like that."

"No, I guess not, Glenn."

"But why would Ernst do it?"

"You tell me why Poley did it and I'll tell you why Ernst did."

Pause. "I don't know what to think, Phil. Two of the seven of us gone. I just can't believe it. What kind of a meeting will we have next year?"

"A pretty gloomy one, if there are any of us left."

"Phil, you don't really think——"

"No, Glenn. I really don't. But I think it ought to be checked out. I'm going to do all I can. If anything turns up, I'll let you know."

I went out to Mollinauer's place of business first, feeling the dread parallel between this and the visit to Baxter, Baxter, Stamper and McGowan. On this day the friendly, good-looking young men in the conservative business suits were in a huddle off to one side of the showroom floor and didn't even see me come in. Well, I couldn't blame them. It had probably shaken them pretty badly. I headed for the office toward the rear, beyond which was the repair department. The eyes of the girl at the desk there were red-rimmed. She said Stanley Burmeister was handling the place to-day, that Mr. Burmeister was really the assistant manager, but now that Mr. Mollinauer . . .

Her eyes welled with tears again and it was all she could do to tell me to go into the inner office, Mr. Burmeister was there.

Stanley Burmeister could have been Ernst Mollinauer's brother. He was large, pink-faced, and at the moment a little dazed and vacant-eyed, staring at the floor. He saw my feet first, and then his eyes slid up to my face. He got up.

"Good morning," he said. He tried to smile.

"My name is Philip DeMoss. I knew Mr. Mollinauer quite well. I'd like to ask you a few questions."

"Of course." He ran a trembling hand over his bald head. "Sit down, sit down." When I was seated, he said, "Men from the police department were here a little while ago." He shook his head. "It's a ghastly business. The questions they asked!"

"They were only trying to do their job," I said gently. "I suppose they asked you about Rose Mollinauer."

"They tried to make me say Ernst and Rose didn't get along." His face became bitter. "Two fine people like that. Nobody ever got along better than Ernst and Rose. Nobody. Even my wife and I never had what they had. And how they can think . . ." He trailed off, shaking his head. "I just don't understand it."

Suddenly he said, "Would you mind closing the door?" When I sat there startled for a moment, he added, "Please."

I closed the door softly and no sooner was it closed than he opened a drawer, brought out a fifth of whisky and two glasses. "Join me?"

I thought it would make him feel less guilty about it if I did, and besides I felt I could stand a drink anyway, so I let him pour one for me. We got chaser water from the corner cooler.

"Haven't I seen you before?" He studied my face as if seeing it for the first time since I entered the room. "You've been here—you were here only the other day talking to Ernst."

"By the Sunbeam Rapier," I said.

"Sure, I remember." He smiled, leaned against the cooler. "I try never to forget a face. Ernst was the best one for that, though. I only try where he was successful. He was a wonderful man, Ernst was. A wonderful man to work with. I owe everything I've got to him. And now he's gone. It just doesn't seem possible."

"I know." I finished my drink. Then I said, "Look, I know this might sound peculiar, but I want to know if you noticed anything odd about Ernst during the past week."

He nodded. "The police wanted to know that too." Sighing, he said, "The whole past week was odd, Ernst not being here and all."

"He wasn't here?"

"Nope. And that wasn't like Ernst at all. He was always the first one here and the last one to go home, or so it seemed. But he wasn't even here for almost a week."

The alarm bells that had started ringing when I had awakened were now making sharp, jangling noises in my head. The thing was following the same pattern as with Poley McGowan!

Burmeister said, "The last time I saw him was last Tuesday morning. I'd just come in myself and was talking with the boys, yakking about quotas and giving them a little pepping up—these young kids, you've got to prop them up all the time or they think they're in the wrong business—when I saw Ernst pull up into the lot next door in his Zephyr. He sat there for a long time and we were all looking at him, wondering why he didn't get out. Then he opened the door, got out, and that's when it happened."

"What happened?"

"Why, this little dog came along and started barking at him. You'd have thought the dog was going to take a bite out of him, and if Ernst had wanted to he could have kicked the pooch to kingdom come. But Ernst, he wouldn't do anything like that. Not Ernst. He liked dogs; cats, too." For a moment Stanley Burmeister was lost in contemplating something in the past and his eyes seemed to film over. But then he went on, "Then Ernst, he got back in the car. We thought maybe he was afraid of the dog or something and was going to wait until it went away. But no, he just started up the car and got out of there. That's the last time any of us down here saw him."

"Didn't he call or anything?"

"Oh, sure. He called every day, several times a day. He wanted reports on this and that. And we called him. He was O.K. He said

36

he was just taking a rest at home. Even joked about it. And then last night this had to happen."

"Did you tell the police all this?"

"Oh, only about Ernst not being here, seeing him drive in and out last Tuesday. I didn't say anything about the dog." He looked embarrassed. "I don't know why I should mention it now."

Burmeister went over to the desk and poured himself another drink, offered me one. But I turned him down. I had other things to do. I said, "Tell me, do you know where Mrs. Mollinauer's mother lives? I think it's in Pacoima somewhere."

"Sure, sure." He reached into a drawer, brought out a thick address book. "Here it is. Mrs. Loretta Bailey. Lives on Amboy Avenue." He gave me the number and then sat down heavily on his chair. "I think I'll finish the bottle. Sure you won't join me?"

I told him I knew how he felt and when I left I closed the door behind me. A man is entitled to drink in peace and private on a day like this.

Before I went out to Pacoima, I called Selma. She told me Jake Hardy had called from San Benuto and that he wanted me to call him. I did. Jake was always at the waterworks, so I had no difficulty locating him.

"Prez," he wheezed when I got him on the line, "what's all this about ol' Ernst?" He didn't sound like himself and I wondered why for a moment. Then I thought I knew: he was a little drunk. Well, he was his own boss and he knew his job; it was nothing to me. I told him what I knew. He said it was just about the same as he'd heard on the radio. He said point-blank Rose couldn't have done it.

"What does it mean, Prez?" he asked then.

That "Prez" bit rankled me a little, but I was in no mood to argue. "I don't know, Jake. If I find out what it means, I'll let you know."

He said gloomily, "The club's getting wrecked."

"Looks that way. I heard you thought Poley wasn't himself at the dinner."

"You think he was, Prez?"

"He seemed all right to me, Jake. What's your opinion of Ernst Mollinauer? Think he was different, too?"

"Oh, hell no. Ernst was his usual self."

We chatted a little more and then I drove out to Pacoima. Mrs. Bailey lived in a modern ranch-style house between two other modern ranch-style houses of the same design, but with variations. Her house was a pastel pink. The one on the right was an off-white, the one on the left a pastel brown. From a distance they looked like a brick of Neapolitan ice cream.

Mrs. Bailey was a thin woman on the far side of fifty, her hair was steel gray, her face the color of putty, and she showed signs of having been physically shaken by the news.

At first she didn't want to let me in. She said she had told the police everything she knew and that if I was a reporter I was wasting my time. I finally convinced her I was a friend of Ernst's, and we went inside.

"I know what you want to know," she said. "You want to know if Rose was having trouble with Ernst. Well, she wasn't." She sat in an easy chair and I sat on a davenport. I could hear children's voices from somewhere else in the house.

"Why did Rose bring the children here then, Mrs. Bailey?"

"Ernst was feeling ill, that's all. Rose said she thought it would be better if I had the kids for a few days."

"Did she say what was wrong with him?"

"Only that he was nervous." She wouldn't meet my eyes. What or how much she was concealing I could only guess.

"Do you have any idea why Ernst should do what he did?"

"No, I don't, Mr.— What did you say your name was?"

"DeMoss. Philip DeMoss. Ernst and I belong to the same alumni club. We graduated from Dorchester College together in nineteen forty-two."

"Oh."

"He was a friend of mine." I told her about Poley, about the parallel in the deaths.

"I didn't know about that." She studied her hands. I let her think. Finally, she said, "I'll tell you something I didn't tell anybody else."

"What is that, Mrs. Bailey?"

"Rose was scared of Ernst."

"Scared, Mrs. Bailey? Why?"

Her face worked in anguish. "Oh, I don't know. Ernst was a fine man, a fine man, a fine, upstanding young man. He was smart and good and I couldn't get it out of Rose why she felt that way."

"Rose was acting odd then, is that it?"

"Yes," she said, nodding, finding a handkerchief and dabbing at her eyes. "Rose wasn't herself. I don't know why. She wouldn't tell me. And now they've got her in the hospital and they won't let anybody see her. It's terrible."

"I sympathize, Mrs. Bailey. I know Rose and I know it's awfully hard for her right now."

"Why don't they let her go? I told them she could come and stay here with me. She wouldn't want to be away from the kids.

As it is, I can't even talk to her, tell her they're all right. Why do they do things like this? There's nothing wrong with Rose! I know my own daughter. She shouldn't be kept there. She's not—insane." Her head came forward and she commenced sobbing. I tried to comfort her the best I could, but when I left her she was still crying and I regretted the necessity of having had to upset her.

On the way back to the city I called Selma again. She said Herb Lincoln had called and I should call him right away. I did.

"Phil," he said in his crisp, professional voice, "I want you to come down to the hospital right away. I've been holding out on you a little and I think we ought to work together on this."

"What's happened, Herb?"

"That gardener—Davenport—wasn't so wrong as we thought." Immediately my thoughts began gyrating again. He went on: "All I can say right now is it's mighty strange."

"What is it?"

"I'd carry on myself, but since we started talking about it together at Poley's, we might as well continue."

"O.K., Herb. I'll be right there."

"Also," he added, "two heads might be safer than one."

That made me shudder a little.

FIVE

I asked for Dr. Lincoln at the information desk. The girl there asked me who I was and when I told her she said he was expecting me in the administrator's office. I went there at once.

Herb was standing at a long window looking down at the cars in the parking lot when I entered. He turned around and I saw a disturbed Herb Lincoln. His hawklike face was drawn. His lips were pressed close together, his eyes looked determined, almost angry.

He said, "Close the door." It was an order. Normally it would have made me a little angry, but there was none of the usual ease about him. It had been replaced by something of a sense of outrage. So I went back to the door and closed it. I didn't wait for him to ask me to sit down.

Herb remained standing and looking down at me from across the administrator's desk. I wanted to say something, anything, because his eyes are rather hypnotic and piercing anyway, and he was certainly setting me on edge. But I calmed myself. All in good time, I told myself. Give the guy a chance. But I hadn't any idea of what he was going to say, which direction he was going.

"I've been trying to get you for the past couple hours," he said. "Your office girl said you told her you might not be in."

"I called in. She told me you called."

"What have you been doing?"

"Two of us gone," I said. "I thought it was more than coincidence, so I was trying to find out why."

"How far did you get?"

"Herb," I said, piqued now, "you said you had something."

"Later, Phil. Tell me about what you've been doing."

I told him, starting with the phone call to Anne and the alarm bells in my head. I told him about Glenn Klock's call, about how Lula thought there was a conspiracy to do away with the alumni group.

"Then I went out to Mollinauer's showroom."

Herb nodded. "You found out he hadn't been there since last Tuesday, I suppose."

"That's right. How did you know?"

"Never mind. Go on."

I told him what Stanley Burmeister told me, including the part about the dog. Herb seemed interested in that. He almost smiled. Then I told him about going to see Ernst's mother-in-law.

"And I forgot. I got a call from Jake Hardy to phone him. So I did."

"What did he have to say?"

"Nothing much. He said he thought Ernst was his usual self at the meeting, which was different from what he thought about Poley."

Herb wanted to know about that, so I told him about the talk I'd had with Cliff and Ernst at the salesroom, and in the course of telling about that I worked back to Davenport.

"That Davenport," I said, shaking my head. "I didn't get a thing out of him. He got all upset when I started asking him about how Poley acted during the week he was at home."

"I know. Ellen McGowan told him not to say anything."

I looked at him squarely. "You've been doing a little investigating of your own, is that it?"

"I called Ellen a little while ago."

I brought out my pipe and filled it as I said, "You said you were holding out on me. Now it's your turn. What have you been doing?"

He sat down in the administrator's chair, folded his long fingers in front of him, a powerful, magnetic man. I would have trusted him with my entire nervous system and everything else thrown in. I'm sure that's the way most people felt about him.

40

"When two fine men go the way Poley and Ernst went, it's more than coincidence." He paused, his eyes flashing fire. "They were killed, Phil."

"Killed?" I was shaken. "But how could they have been killed? They killed themselves—both of them."

He said grimly, quietly, "They were driven to it, Phil."

"Driven to it?" I said foolishly.

"Yes. Driven to it by an aura of fear and hate." His eyes were far away. "They were suddenly alien to humanity."

I could not talk. This was too close to the crazy things I had been thinking.

Herb leaned forward on the desk and said earnestly, "Phil, I like you. I think you've got a good head on your shoulders. I also think we see pretty much eye to eye on things. And I know you're vitally interested in this."

"I'm not only interested, Herb, I'm concerned. But this business about being alien . . ."

He waved a hand to shush me. "You'll understand in a moment." Then he leaned back, studying me. "What I'm going to say to you is a violation of medical ethics and confidence. Now don't say anything. I just want you to know I've weighed it, the pros and cons, and I think I can trust you with it—in fact, I think you might be downright helpful. Especially if it turns out that Poley died the way Ernst did, and I think he did."

"In an aura of fear?"

He nodded. "And hate."

I felt ridiculous because he was so far ahead of me. "This aura —do you know what causes it?"

"Something. Either of this world or another." He smiled wryly. "I feel as if I've gone off the deep end when I say a thing like that, but believe me there's a reason."

My heart was beating rapidly. What had Herb run onto?

"I talked to Rose Mollinauer, Phil. I talked with her for a long time. She wasn't able to talk normally, so I arranged to interrogate her under narcosynthesis. I thought it was important and I was able to do it without too much trouble."

"What did she say?"

He slapped his hands on the desk and stood up. "It's the damndest thing I ever heard." He turned and walked to the window again, looking out pensively. If I hadn't had my pipe in my teeth, I would have chewed my nails.

"You've got to get it the way I did to get the picture. So listen. Rose said that last Tuesday morning Ernst got up as he usually did. They sleep in twin beds. She got up, too, and went to the kitchen. Nothing was wrong at this point. But Ernst usually goes in to take a look at the kids before he comes out for breakfast. This is after he uses the bathroom and makes himself ready for the day. She said she heard him humming, heard the splash of water, even said a few things to him and he answered. Then she heard him leave the bathroom, go to the bedroom, get dressed and then start for the kitchen. It was at this point that she recalled hearing the kids in their room making noises that kids do in the early morning. They're just little kids."

"Somewhere under six."

"The next thing she knew the kids were screaming, as if something terrible was happening to them. She thought they'd fallen out the window or had somehow caught on fire or something. Anyway, she ran to the room." Herb turned to me. His eyes were bright and fearful. "There was Ernst."

"What was he doing?"

"Nothing. Absolutely nothing. He was just standing there in the middle of the nursery, staring openmouthed at the children. They were screaming their heads off at him."

"Why, for heaven's sake?"

"At first Rose was so concerned for the kids that she didn't really notice Ernst. She says she ran over to them, grabbed them up and tried to quiet them, but they wouldn't be quiet. Then she turned and looked at Ernst."

"What was wrong with him?"

"Nothing was wrong with him. He was standing there with a hurt look on his face. That's all. He wasn't even moving."

I scratched my head. My pipe had gone out, but I didn't care. I just didn't understand it at all. I said, "I don't get it, Herb."

Herb was staring at me, through me. It was almost frightening, seeing him like that, but I suddenly realized he was living the scene, remembering Rose as she told it to him, as he drew it out of her piece by piece while she was under the influence of the drug.

"It was then," he said, "that she sensed it, the terrible fear. There was nothing wrong with Ernst. Nothing at all. Yet as she sat there on the bed with her two children in her arms she was terrified of him, really terrified. Then she found herself screaming at him, telling him to go away, to get out of there."

"What was it, Herb?"

"I don't know. Not really." He sighed and walked over to the desk and sat on an edge of it. "That was only the beginning. She saw him—poor Ernst—back out of the room with a look of utter disbelief on his face. Disbelief and agony. She heard him walk down the hall, get his coat and go out the door. In a few minutes her heart stopped racing, her cold sweat was gone. Then she sat there for a long time with the children, trying to understand what had happened to them. Do you get the picture?"

"Yes. Do you think she's——"

"Telling the truth?" He shot me a glance. "I know she's telling the truth, Phil. I felt a little of what she felt myself."

"You mean the fear?"

"Something like it. But with me it was more loathing. Let me tell you more. Ernst Mollinauer, now a confused man, went downstairs and got his car out of the apartment garage. He drove to work. On the way there perhaps another experience or two, just like the previous one, happened. He got to work, started to get out of the car, when this dog started barking at him. Do you see it now, Phil? Do you see the horrible thing that has happened to him?"

"Everybody's afraid of him?"

"Exactly. So he never went in the showroom. He just stepped back in his car and drove home. Rose said she hoped it was him returning when she heard the step on the stairs. She felt terrible about what she'd done, screaming the way she had, and she wanted to talk to him about it. But even as she neared the door, she sensed this thing, this fear and loathing as he opened the door and walked through it. Then it was back in full force, the indescribable panic again. She backed away, put her hand over her mouth to keep from crying out. Ernst turned quickly and went into their bedroom, closing the door. After that it wasn't so bad —the panic, that is. They talked through the door. Rose said she thought there was something wrong with her, but each time she tried to enter the bedroom, she found she couldn't do it. Ernst then told her he experienced nothing, that he felt perfectly normal.

"The trouble was with her, then? No, it couldn't be, not if others reacted, the kids, the dog . . ."

"No, the trouble was with Ernst all right, but somehow he didn't feel any different."

"I see. So she took the children to her mother's place."

"She said that Ernst suggested that. She said she tried to figure it out, all the way to Pacoima, but she couldn't make head or tail of it. When she got back, she found that Ernst had eaten his breakfast and scurried back into the bedroom just before she let herself in. It went on then like that for days, except that she shut herself in the bathroom while Ernst moved into the children's room and slept across their two beds there at night. She found it difficult to get rid of the anxiety she felt around the house, but she was successful when she got out of it and went to the store to buy things. She slept in their bedroom, they talked across the apartment, she got meals for him. They thought that time would wear it out, whatever it was, but every morning they'd go through the same thing again—Ernst getting ready to go to work, everything seemingly normal, only to find suddenly that Rose felt the same way still."

I filled my pipe as Herb was silent. I thought of the incredible shifting of two people in an apartment, avoiding each other, experiencing Rose's feeling of anguish and pain, Ernst's bewilderment and perhaps panic within himself at the thought of never being able to face people again, for above all things Ernst was a loving man, not just Rose, and his kids, but cats and dogs just as Stanley Burmeister had said. It must have been a horrible time for him.

"So," I said, "Late last night he couldn't stand it any more. He jumped from the bedroom window."

"Not exactly," Herb said. "As the days went on, they became almost rational about it. Rose wanted to call in a doctor, but Ernst said no doctor would be able to come near him, no living thing could stand him. He made her promise not to subject him to that, not to let anyone know. They lived the week hoping it would end as suddenly as it had begun. They even tried to be normal. He'd answer the phone, Rose scurrying out of the room. Sometimes, especially in the morning, Rose simply had to get out of the house. She said she thought about not going back. She said if Ernst hadn't been her husband and the father of her children, she might not have. It must have been pretty terrible.

"Anyway, she was asleep last night when she heard Ernst at the door. And this is the awful part, Phil. You must remember that Ernst loved his wife, that he was a creature of the flesh, in order to understand that he could not endure this very long. Perhaps something did go wrong inside him at the end. Who knows? How much can a man take? Anyway, Rose said he barged into the room, tried to take her in his arms, telling her how much he loved her and how they could not go on the way they had. But his proximity only produced an even more overpowering sensation of revulsion that she tried with all her heart to dispel. But it was no use, and she could not stand it. She had to scream. She couldn't help it.

"She said he stood there listening to her for a long moment. Then he uttered a cry and ran for the French windows. He crashed through them and over a little railing on the outside. The rest you know."

Herb let me sit there for a long time, letting me digest it, bit by bit. My hands were cold. The room was cold. I even found myself for the moment hating him for having told me about it, for it somehow ruined the picture I had of Ernst and Rose. A

44

storybook happiness torn to shreds in a little more than a few days.

If Rose was to be believed, that is. But of course she was to be believed. So if Herb was to be believed, then. I looked up and found his eyes on mine. Cold, professional. Yet in their depths there was resolution. But then Herb was a militant man, a man of such resolution.

"I know you're wondering if I'm telling the truth," he said. "You don't have to believe me. I have trouble enough believing it myself. If it weren't for several other factors, I might not believe it at all."

"Other factors?"

"Yes. Two men, Colin Faraday and John Smithers, were on the ambulance detail here last night. They were summoned to the scene by police. When they reached it, they witnessed a strange thing. Instead of the usual crowd around the injured man, there was a ring. No one was within twenty feet of him. The police had not even put a blanket over him. The men in the patrol car said they didn't know why, but each of the two men in the patrol car blames the other. Neither will own up to the fact that they had a sudden and violent antipathy for what lay in the street.

"Now Faraday and Smithers are used to such things. Yet it was almost more than they could bear to put Ernst on the stretcher. Also, I might say at this point, there were two different reactions. Faraday's was fear; Smithers' was hate. An important point, Phil. In the crowd, I also imagine—and this is only guesswork— there must also have been two reactions: one of fear and the other of hatred. I talked with Faraday and Smithers, Phil. I talked to them because Ernst was a friend of mine. This difference in reaction came out because Faraday and Smithers are also my friends and told me what they might not have told someone else. And they are as unable to tell me why they had these feelings as Rose is.

"I did something else, too, Phil. Since Ernst was dead on arrival here, he was taken to the morgue. I wanted to see what the sight of him would do to me, if I would have a reaction, so I went to the morgue. I asked to see Ernst Mollinauer."

"And?"

"And I loathed him when I saw him."

"You loathed Ernst Mollinauer?" This I positively could not understand.

"He was dead, but it was still with him, whatever it was. It wasn't strong, but I sensed it. Loathing, revulsion. Not exactly hatred. The attendant remarked about it. He felt it, too, you see.

45

Now get this: A little while ago, just before calling you, I went there again. This time I did not loathe him any more."

His eyes glittered as he looked at me and said, "I think Poley went through the same thing. I think that's why he didn't go to his office. I think that's why he walked into the ocean."

"You said you talked to Ellen about it. What did she say?"

"She says she'll see us at"—He looked at his wrist watch—"three fifteen. It's three now."

SIX

Ellen McGowan was very much in control of herself when she met us at the door. She was again gracious, beautiful and feminine, and her eyes were warm and seemingly untroubled. The only marks of recent strain were the dark shadows under her eyes and a little paler than normal cast to her skin. Of course she had never been what one might call lighthearted and gay, but she could have been gaunt, drawn and depressed, and she was none of these.

"I'm so glad you could come," she said, ushering us into the spacious living room. "I'm alone and we can talk. I'm interested in what you were telling me, Dr. Lincoln." Her eyes jumped to mine. "And Dr. Lincoln has told me you conducted an inquiry of your own about Poley, Phil. I want you to know I appreciate it, and I want to hear about anything you have discovered, too."

"Thank you. I'll be glad to, Ellen."

"I was never Dr. Lincoln to you or Poley," Herb said. "I want you to call me Herb. I'd feel uncomfortable if you didn't."

She smiled. "All right, Herb. I didn't know how you felt." She seated us comfortably, asked us if we wanted a drink, but Herb declined and, seeing that he wanted to get on with it, so did I. "You were saying there was a parallel in Ernst's death, Herb."

"Yes." He told her briefly what had happened, recounting in less detail than he had told me, about what Rose had told him. During the telling of it, I saw Ellen's face gradually become paler and paler. Finally, at the end of it, she said she wanted a drink, even if we didn't, and Herb suggested then she make it two and looked at me. I said make it three.

"What I want to know," Herb said, when we were back with drinks in our hands, "is how really similar the cases were. Did Poley act the way Ernst did? Were you affected the same way?"

Ellen spent a long time looking at her drink. I could see she was recalling it all, trying to work out a way to tell it without being

46

too affected by it. But there was no way and she must have finally decided that, for she said.

"There's not a lot of difference. It just started the Monday morning after the dinner. We'd spent a wonderful Sunday together, Poley and I and the kids. We flew up the coast and had a picnic lunch at Davenport Landing. There are little coves and big breakers there and the children love it. Then we flew back and spent a quiet evening at home—oh, some people dropped by, but other than that it was quiet."

"Do you remember who dropped by, Ellen?"

"Oh, I don't remember. The days are so mixed up in my mind now. But I do know Poley seemed happy and I know I was. He'd never been nicer, he'd never had more fun with the kids or been more attentive to me."

"It started the next morning then," Herb said. He wanted to get her off their last Sunday night together, I could see that.

"Yes. He simply came out to the kitchen. I was terrified before I even turned to see him——"

"Before you *saw* him?"

"Yes. I didn't know what was wrong with me. At first I thought I was going to faint, my heart was beating so fast. My ears started roaring and I didn't know what was wrong. The feeling grew. It was sheer panic and I wanted to run. Then I turned and saw Poley and he started to come over to me, asking me what was wrong." She bit a lip, tears welled in her eyes and she turned away. "I had vowed never to tell anyone about this."

"You must now, Ellen. It's important. Something's wrong and we've got to know what it is."

She nodded. "Yes, I can see that." She took a deep breath and looked at me. "Davenport told me how curious you were, Phil. I couldn't know how much you guessed. I hoped none of it. Up to today I considered it a sort of sickness with us and I certainly didn't want to air any of it, as I've said. I had told Davenport, who witnessed a lot of it, not to say anything to anyone. To my knowledge he hasn't."

"He wouldn't talk to me," I confessed.

"Davenport's a good man." She drew a handkerchief from her pocket and blew her nose gently. "It was just as it was with Rose. Poley couldn't understand my panic, my loathing, my fear. Of course I couldn't understand it myself. Every time he came near me, I'd scream. It was frightful and not at all like me. Poley knew that and said he was going to call our doctor, but before he could get to the phone, Terry came into the kitchen. I'll never forget it. Terry said, 'What's for breakfast, Mom?' Then he took one look at his father. From then on it was frightful."

"He was afraid, too," Herb said.

"No. He wasn't afraid. His eyes became the eyes of an animal at bay. He clenched his teeth. Then he rushed at his father and commenced hitting him as hard as he could. He actually knocked him down, so vicious was his attack. Poley tried to get Terry away from him and in doing so his forearm was exposed to Terry's teeth." Ellen shuddered. "Terry sank his teeth into Poley's arm and Poley cried out with pain."

"Terry was like a terrified animal," I said. "Even though they're afraid, some rodents——" I shut my mouth.

I don't think Ellen knew what I'd said. She went on, "Poley managed to disengage Terry, and in the scuffle—you can never know how hideous it was—Terry slid across the floor. Just then Patricia and Clarence came running in. When they saw what was going on, they stood there screaming at the top of their lungs. It was awful. Then Davenport came in. I'll never forget the loathing in his eyes. And that was so unlike gentle, loving Davenport. I don't believe he ever had an evil thought in his life. Of course I don't think Poley did either. Or the children. How do you account for it, Doctor—Herb?"

"I don't know," Herb said. "What happened then?"

"Poley left the house and got in the car and drove away. I don't know where he went or what he did. I called a doctor because the children were so upset by it all, made them promise to say nothing to him when he arrived. But he could tell they'd been through something and so had I. He left some tranquilizers for me and some medicine for the kids. Within an hour or so they were feeling chipper again, so I thought it would be all right for them to go to school. I didn't know when Poley'd be home."

"He never tried to go to the office, did he?"

"No. They called and I said he wasn't feeling well, hoping he wouldn't try going there. Of course I know now what it was, but I was frantic with worry then, and I don't remember actually what I did or who called."

"You didn't tell the doctor about it?"

"No." She shook her head. "I tried to think of how I could phrase it, what I could tell him, but it was no use. I thought we were all losing our minds." She added sadly, "Poor Rose. Perhaps it was even worse for her, being in an apartment. At least we could get out of the house here. It was all right if we didn't get near Poley, but closer than say twenty feet and something terrible happened to us all. Poley was miserable. He spent hours out in the garden in the sun trying to think it out. He used the pool. But nothing made any difference. I don't see how he was able to carry on with his office work."

"Things went on like this until he decided to end it, is that it?"

"No, it didn't. I kept the children in one part of the house and I gave them pink medicine the doctor gave me for them. They slept most of the time they weren't in school. I was glad they did, Poley and I being at our wits' end. The tranquilizers helped me, but they didn't reduce the way I felt about my husband when he was near me. On the third—no, it was the fourth day, Thursday—Poley started to drink. You understand there wasn't anything wrong with him—only with his effect on people. He felt the better for it and I didn't try to stop him. With a few drinks in him, he minimized it in his mind and tried to go to work on Friday. But he came back dejected and started drinking in earnest. He said he stopped for a paper and created a disturbance. It seems one man wanted to hit him and another backed away in horror and fell off the curb into the street and was nearly run over by a car.

"That trip seemed to do something to him, and that weekend he didn't care what he looked like, what he did. On Sunday he came to some sort of decision, walked out of here drunk—if you can imagine Poley drunk. None of us had been near him for days; I didn't know where he was going. But I was afraid for him. I thought perhaps he'd go look up one of his friends and I was afraid too what that would do for him. But he seemed unmindful of his condition."

"Where did he go?"

"I don't know. I guess he just took a long walk."

"And he didn't get into trouble?"

"No. You see—well, he came back jubilant. Whatever it was, it was gone. Nobody hated him any more, including his family."

"He was all right again?" This was contradictory.

Ellen smiled wryly. "Yes. Oh, he wasn't much to look at when he came back, but this—this horrible aura was gone. He was unshaven, unkempt. He looked like something from Skid Row. But I didn't care. I was happy it was over. I loved him again. We didn't want to do anything to change it. He kept the same soiled clothes on and got gloriously drunk. I—I'm afraid I drank a lot myself. You simply can't know what it's like to have your man back again."

"But it was on Monday that he——" Herb started to say.

"Yes. He got up and we went through exactly what we had gone through the previous Monday. He had it again. I saw the surprise, the disappointment, the hurt in his eyes, the pain. But there was nothing I could do about it. I couldn't even tell him I loved him because there was something about him that made me hate him."

"So," Herb said, "it was the last straw."

"Yes. He couldn't stand the thought of it any more."

49

There were lengthening shadows in the living room, and from somewhere deep in the house came the sound of a motor hum, probably the refrigerator. Otherwise it was as still as death, and in the place that had been Poley's there was an odor of decay and hate and fear, except that it was only in my mind. But once there had been really hate and fear here in this house, just as there had been hate and fear in the Mollinauer apartment.

Ellen broke the spell I was under by saying, "Now I've told you how it was. You're a doctor, Herb, and a good one. Suppose you tell me what happened."

Herb got up and walked to the wide windows that overlooked the lawn and the steps down to the pool. He stood there for a long time deep in thought. Then he turned and said, "I have a theory, but in order to understand it, you must know something of the physiology of fear and rage." He stroked his chin contemplatively, his bushy eyebrows drawn down hard in concentration. He looked very much the doctor and I was proud of him, proud that he had asked me to help him, though I felt that I had been of little help up to this point. Still I was there and I was eager to get to the bottom of it and then decide on a course of action, for Herb did nothing without a reason, without a goal, and I knew his analysis would provide the solution, the action, the reason, the goal.

"In your case, Ellen, the cortex of your brain was somehow stimulated to perceive a threat," Herb said, starting to pace the floor, talking as if to a group of students in an amphitheater. "I'm not prepared to say precisely how. The cortex, so stimulated, sent a stimulus down the sympathetic branch of your autonomic nervous system to the adrenal glands." He stopped and faced Ellen. "In your case, in Rose's, the glands secreted the hormone. Your respiration deepened, your heart started to beat more rapidly, your arterial blood pressure rose."

"I was frightened, is that what you're saying?"

"Yes. Your blood was shifted from the stomach and intestines to the heart and nervous system and muscles. The processes in your alimentary canal ceased. Sugar was freed from reserves in your liver, your spleen contracted and discharged its content of concentrated corpuscles, and adrenin was secreted from the adrenal medulla.

"You were scared, Ellen, confronted by a simulated situation which evoked fear. But it was not the same with Terry. In him it evoked rage. But the physiological reaction in either case is much the same. That is important. It gives us a clue of sorts."

Herb tugged at his lower lip for a moment. Then he went on pacing as shadows deepened. "This secreted adrenin cooperated

50

with sympathetic nerve impulses and called forth stored glycogen from the liver, flooding the blood with sugar for use in laboring muscles. It was sent in large supply to the heart, the brain and limbs, and this same blood was rendered more readily coagulable." He continued his walk, nodding his head. "That's the picture. The whole picture. The reason for the effect."

"O.K., Herb," I broke in. "That's the effect. I remember a lot of it from my college textbooks. But the thing is, what caused it in Ellen and Rose, in Faraday and Smithers, in the dog and in everybody else Poley and Ernst came into contact with?"

"No," Herb said. "The problem isn't so much what caused it in them—even in me to a lesser degree when I viewed Ernst's body. The problem is why should it be caused at all, and precisely by Poley and Ernst."

"So you have a theory as to that?" Ellen asked.

"Vaguely. There is much research going on behind closed and barred laboratory doors these days on various types of nerve gas. You will notice that neither Rose nor Ellen said they smelled anything. That would fit the deadly gases we already know about which attack nerves. They are odorless and tasteless and colorless. But this doesn't fit the pattern exactly. This is something different. This is something that doesn't harm the host but stimulates fear and anger in those near him.

"There are such things as substrates, the substances upon which enzymes act. Choline estrase is an enzyme and acetylcholine is a substrate of choline estrase. In order for nerves to function there must be no inhibition of their electrical functions, for they truly do operate like electric wires. The body's prime generator of electricity is acetylcholine. Anything which would inhibit its properties, its abilities, would be deadly. Nerve gas, G-gas do this."

I said, "You're getting pretty far out in left field for me."

Herb smiled. "I'm sorry, Phil. Talking to myself. What I'm saying is that we have a substance similar to nerve gas—we *must* have. Somehow the host body is able to produce this in great quantities, through stimulation, but is itself immune to it. But it isn't the same kind of nerve gas we read about so much in the papers. This one simply attacks the cerebral cortex and simulates the fear and anger patterns there."

"But how does the—the host body as you say—produce this gas?" Ellen wanted to know.

"Maybe through the sweat glands. Perhaps bacteria. Maybe even through exhalation."

I put my two cents in. "This means that Poley and Ernst must have come in contact with something that produced this result."

"That's right, Phil. Somehow they were stimulated. But how? That's the big question. And another thing: If they knew how they were stimulated and with what, we could find an antidote. Intramuscular injections of atrophine sulfate is an antidote for nerve gas. So is pyridine aldoxime methiodide. But I know without even trying that they wouldn't do in these cases because there isn't the same reaction." He hit the palm of one hand with his fist. "If only I knew the stimulus!"

We were silent, each wondering what could have possibly caused Ernst and Poley to become carriers of whatever it was, while others in the same house were not.

Finally Ellen said, "Tell me something, Herb. Do you think this was deliberate?"

"Do you mean do I think somebody did it? My answer is that I don't know. There are loose in the world today many vapors, radiations, new chemicals, reactions—so many things we don't understand, things that haven't been tested. Who can say? It doesn't seem reasonable that anyone would want Poley to experience it, would want to drive him to suicide. Or that someone would want to repeat the same thing with Ernst. I would prefer to think in terms of a catalyst, something accidental. Maybe even extraterrestrial, if need be."

"But if it were a person," Ellen went on, "who would it be? Who would want to do a thing like that?"

"I hope," Herb said, "that we never have to answer that." Then He glanced at his watch. "It's after five. I suggest we call the others in the group and tell them what we have found out. It may be that we're way off base on this thing, but I think it's better to be warned and on guard even though we may be wrong than to be ignorant of what's happening. Then I think we'd better talk to the police."

Ellen told us to use her phone. I called Glenn Klock. He thought I was drunk, but I finally convinced him I wasn't. Then Herb called Clifford Ellis, who was also sceptical. Since Jake Hardy also lived in San Benuto, Cliff said he'd call him and tell him.

When we finished phoning, I said soberly, "If by chance it is somebody in the club, it's got to be Glenn, Cliff or Jake."

Herb grinned. He didn't often do that. But he said, "A mighty big if. But one thing you forgot."

"What's that?"

"It could be you or I. Didn't think of that, did you?"

I confessed I hadn't. But I was sure of one thing. I wasn't the one. That would leave Glenn, Cliff, Jake and Herb. And the thought struck me right then: If it was somebody in our group, who among us would know anything about nerve gases, about such things as the cerebral cortex and the nervous system?

Only Herb Lincoln. Or possibly Glenn Klock.

But the thought of their being responsible was out of the question. I would rather believe it was little flying saucer men. Ridiculous? The whole thing was ridiculous. Or fantastic, a much better word for it. Anyway, I was ready to believe anything, including aliens from a far advanced planet of another star system.

SEVEN

Lieutenant Andrew Grever was a patient man. He listened to Herb Lincoln from beginning to end without showing either approval or disapproval, only putting a question here, a question there. His eyes were tired eyes, blue eyes, but they looked as if they had seen everything, and as they watched Herb and me, I saw there was an alert brain behind them that was weighing everything on a finely adjusted analytical scale. He was a big man, a man with massive shoulders, hair as white as Poley's, and his complexion was ruddy.

When Herb finished, Lieutenant Grever turned to me and asked me what my part in it was. I told him. After that he lit a cigarette and stared across the small room we were in, considering it.

Finally he smiled a little and said to Herb, "Everything you've said could be the truth, Dr. Lincoln. I know one part in fact that really is true—the bit about the officers not covering the body of Mr. Mollinauer. But you'll have to admit what you're saying is unbelievable."

Herb said quietly, "You don't think these things happened?"

Grever said gravely, "Dr. Lincoln, as a physician and surgeon, and as a friend of everybody involved, you had advantages the police department did not. You were able to get Mrs. McGowan to say things to you she wouldn't say to us. You were able to bring Mrs. Mollinauer out of her shock state to talk to her."

I said, "You don't believe they said all that, is that it, Lieutenant?"

"Of course I believe they said it. What I am getting at is you two aren't police officers." He waved a deprecatory hand at us. "Now don't be offended. I'm no doctor or lawyer either. But if you two had been police officers, it would have made a difference. What you have found out would now be a matter of police record and we would have to recognize it. All I can do now is

53

accept your word for what these people said and try to start from there."

Lieutenant Grever sighed and stood up. He was even taller than Herb, who was a good six feet two, and he carried his weight well as he stretched and commenced a little walk back and forth. "You said, Doctor, that you don't know how these men became afflicted. Have you any idea why—or better yet, who is responsible?"

Herb scowled. "We have no more reason to think it is a person than we have to think it was caused by—well, sunspots. The fact that two members of our Forty-two Club are dead perhaps lends credence to the idea of a guilty person, but some chemical or vapor accident could have occurred when we were all together at the dinner and has only recently had time to mature. Bacteria work that way. Maybe others of us have it, maybe we're carrying it with us, and it will mature one of these days."

Now Lieutenant Grever smiled. "But you came to us because you think that it might be some*one* rather than some*thing*."

"It is a possibility," Herb conceded.

"It is also the only angle from which the police department can approach it, the angle of human frailty, Dr. Lincoln. The world is unfortunately filled with it. Now do you think it possible that there might be somebody on the outside, some disgruntled classmate, somebody who flunked out or something who might have suddenly come to hate your group?"

"If there is, I don't know who it could be."

"Does your organization have a treasury?"

"Not much of one. A few dollars."

I explained how we always split the costs of the annual meetings. "There are no dues or anything like that."

Grever nodded. "Those of you in Los Angeles and San Benuto are just a little group, a clique, a small part of the larger Dorchester class of forty-two."

"Yes."

"And no great amount of money is involved."

"Nothing except Poley's and Ernst's insurance money," Herb said. "That will be quite a sum. It will probably go to their wives and children."

The lieutenant looked at me. "How about you, Mr. DeMoss? Do you have any ideas on the subject?"

"I'm a complete blank," I confessed. "I can't see who would gain by what's happened. I just hope it does turn out to be a virus, a bacteria strain, sunspots or little green men. I'd hate to think that anyone in the Forty-two Club——"

"Of course you do," Grever said dryly, sitting down again. "This group now—there are five of you left—do either of you think that any of the others could, by the wildest stretch of your imagination, be the engineer of this thing?"

Herb shook his head. "I don't know who it could be Lieutenant. It would have to be someone who has a special knowledge of this sort. Phil here is a lawyer. Jake Hardy runs a municipal water-works, Clifford Ellis writes books, and Glenn Klock is an officer with an encyclopedia firm. None of them fits."

The lieutenant eyed Herb squarely. "You have special knowledge in the field, Doctor."

"Yes," Herb said slowly, "I suppose I have. All I can say is I would never do a thing like that."

"It was Dr. Lincoln who found out what it was about," I pointed out. "Anyone responsible would certainly not come to the police with it."

"Not unless he was a psychopath," the lieutenant said. "But you speak of someone being responsible. Even murders sometimes are accidental, a gun lying around, poison inadvertently left somewhere, and it looks like murder at first glance. I suppose people have actually been convicted—maybe executed—for less."

"Well, perhaps we have no grounds for thinking premeditation," Herb said, "yet I don't know what else to think. I'm sure Mrs. McGowan and Mrs. Mollinauer didn't want to get rid of their husbands. Why would anyone want to put himself through such a thing in the first place? On the other hand, the accident theory doesn't satisfy me either." He threw his hands in the air, his elbows came down on the tabletop and he pressed his long fingers to his forehead. "I don't know what to think any more. What I need is a good night's sleep."

"We called the others in the group, Lieutenant," I said. "We thought we'd better warn them."

Lieutenant Grever grunted. "You've probably scared them half to death."

"They seemed hard to convince."

"I'm not sure it was the right thing to do. If this is a matter of premeditaion and one of them is the perpetrator, it gives him an in. He knows now that everybody knows about it. Everybody will be watchful."

"Watchful?" I was amused. "Watchful for what?"

Grever didn't answer. He said instead, "What are these other guys like—this Klock, for instance? You said he's something with encyclopedias. Is he a brooding type? Moody? Could you picture him doing something like this?"

I laughed. "Not Glenn Klock. He's too studious, too withdrawn. No, it couldn't be Klock."

"Don't be too sure, Mr. DeMoss. It's the reserved, studious ones you've got to watch out for."

I said bluntly, "Glenn Klock wouldn't hurt a fly."

Grever shrugged. "You know him, of course. How about"— He looked at the names he'd written on a piece of paper—"Jake Hardy?"

"Jake?" His face appeared in my mind. "He drinks a lot, he's a practical man and frankly, Lieutenant, I don't think he'd have the aptitude for it. He wasn't the best student Dorchester ever had."

"Maybe he's jealous of the rest of you."

"For the grades we got at Dorchester?"

"No, for the names you've made for yourself."

Herb said, "Jake Hardy isn't the jealous type, Lieutenant. He's a practical joker, a backslapper, a lodge man. He can be the life of the party when he wants to be. I don't think he would run out of jokes from now to doomsday if you gave him enough to drink."

Grever said stubbornly, "Still, Poley McGowan and Ernst Mollinauer were pretty successful, at least in material things. Jealousy could be a motive in this. But as you say, you know your man. How about Clifford Ellis? Seems to me I've read some of his stuff. Doesn't he write paperbacks?"

"He's written a lot of books," I said. "Some are pretty off-color. He's always attacking the *status quo*."

"Has he communist leanings?"

"I don't think so. I think he gets his kicks out of tearing things down. He's always talking about how terrible everything is, how much better off we'd be if we were all dead. He does it for effect."

"Is that so?" Grever was interested. "Maybe he's decided to carry out his ideas, starting with the club you're in."

"I think he's harmless," Herb said. "Talks too much, if you ask me. If he could kill somebody with a book, he might do it, but I don't think he'd do it with any overt act."

"If," Grever said, "an overt act was involved."

There was more. It seemed that we discussed every possibility, every angle. Herb and I were both worn out when it was over, and Lieutenant Grever didn't look exactly refreshed. I dropped Herb at his place and then went home to my own apartment. It was too late to call Selma—even at her home—so I had a nightcap, only confused myself by thinking about it all some more, and then went to bed. I slept like a rock.

In the morning I woke refreshed and optimistic. Herb and I had done the right thing. We'd found out something and we had taken it to the right place—to the police. Maybe it was escape I was feeling, that the whole thing was no longer my responsibility, that experienced investigators were now on the job. Whatever it was, it stayed with me and I went to the office and waded into what had become a backlog.

"Well," Selma said with a little snort I couldn't help but catch the significance of, "you're back on the job." Selma Livingston had been with me a long time; she can get away with things like that.

I said, "I feel the office has been in good hands."

"Thank you. You're looking better. No longer the weight of the world on your shoulders."

"Did I look bad?"

"A thousand miles away."

"Well, I am back then. Let's get with it, shall we?"

"I've been with it, Mr. DeMoss."

"If you want to stay with it then, Miss Livingston, I'd suggest we commence work. What's first on the agenda?"

"I forgot you wouldn't know." She turned and flounced out of the office for the little outer office. I didn't mind. Sometimes I thought she was more conscientious about the business of Philip DeMoss, Attorney at Law, than Philip DeMoss was. She came back in with enough paper work to keep me going for a week. She laid it all out neatly. Then we went to work.

I had lunch with Anne. I didn't know how much to tell her, and I certainly didn't want to go into all the gruesome details, but Anne Whiting has a way of getting things out of me and before I knew it she had the whole story.

"It's ghastly," she said. "Perfectly ghastly." She looked very angry. "How anybody could do a thing like that to anybody else is completely beyond me."

"We don't know that anybody did. We don't know that much about it."

"If there was just one person—if this had happened to Poley alone or to Ernst, then you could say that. But that it could happen to two people, that's something else again."

"You feel it's deliberate and premeditated?"

"On the part of a person or persons unknown. Isn't that the right way to say it?"

"Yes, if it's true. But I repeat that we don't know that it's true. I still think it could be sunspots."

Now Anne was thinking. She is beautiful. Her eyes are the very shade of deep blue I can't ignore. The way she puts up her dark brown hair, the way the light shines on it to bring out a deep copper glint, makes me defenceless. Even without her moving I find I love her, the way she's made, her neck, her shoulders. But I'm just butter when she does move, and it's hard for me to resist giving in to her every whim and mood. Now I didn't want her troubled by this problem. I didn't want her troubled by anything.

Her fine eyebrows were brought down, her face had a stern look and her even white teeth sank into the redness of her lower lip. So I said, "Now don't you start trying to figure it out. The police are in charge now. I've washed my hands of it. It's not my job or yours."

She said in surprise, "You mean you're giving up?"

"I mean I'm not devoting any more time to it. After all, I'm a lawyer, not a private eye or a police detective."

"Phil, how can you say that? Didn't Poley or Ernst mean any more to you than that?"

"Of course they did, but if either of them had had appendicitis, I wouldn't undertake the operation."

"But this isn't like that! Who knows the people in the Forty-two Club better than you and Herb?"

I was half angry. "What more could Herb or I do?"

"Think," she said. "Think hard."

"I've thought so hard about it I'm numb with it."

"You haven't thought hard enough about it, that's your trouble. If you had, you'd know who's responsible."

"If," I said wearily, "it was a member of the alumni club, *if* it was premeditated, and *if* it's possible somebody actually did do it."

"Of course someone did it!"

"Oh? Will you please tell the court, Miss Whiting, how you managed to arrive at this conclusion?"

"Oh, don't be so frosty." She reached for a spoon and proceeded to eat the ice cream that had been brought for dessert.

"All right, so I won't be frosty. Now tell me how you know."

"Intuition."

"Intuition?" I had to laugh. "That would never stand up in court."

"Don't be so cocksure, Philip DeMoss. A woman's intuition can be a powerful thing. It knows no rules. It takes short cuts. Take my mother, for example."

"You have a lovely mother, Anne."

"You remember those Minute Mysteries? They'd give you the picture of a crime, tell you the story of it, give you all the clues, give you a little background of the people and their movements just before, during and after the murder?"

"Sure, I remember them."

"Well, my mother was a whiz. She'd figure them out without all the clues, even halfway through sometimes."

"She must be a pretty remarkable woman to do that."

"And when we'd ask her how in the world she did it—and she was always right—she'd say she didn't know how. She just knew, that's all. Intuition."

I gave up. "All right, Anne. What does your intuition tell you about this? If you are your mother's daughter, you ought to be able to do it."

"Oh, I don't have the answer. I just feel that someone did it, that's all. Somebody in your club. I don't know who. Maybe I'll get intuitive about who it is later."

"Uh-huh. But you can't put somebody in jail on intuition."

"No, but you can stop him from doing it any more."

"Him, Annie?"

"Of course. How could it be a woman?"

"How about Lula, Glenn Klock's wife? They've been married for I don't know how long and they don't have any children."

Anne said, "I know about that. She said how much she and Glenn wanted children when I saw her at the dinner. But I don't follow you."

"Figure it this way. The two men in the Forty-two Club with the most children are dead. Lula envied their wives for the children they had and she didn't have. So she got even with them by killing their husbands."

"Herb Lincoln has a child and nothing happened to him."

"Give her time. Lula likes to let a week go by in between."

"Sometimes," Anne said, "I hate you."

"We don't have to worry, Jake Hardy, Clifford Ellis and I. We don't have any children. We're not even married."

Anne said tartly, "Just for that I'm not going to marry you. You speak of the bachelor state as something highly to be desired."

"It's only keeping Lula away. Why, once we got married and had a houseful of kids, Lula Klock would be around to put the hex on me and there I'd go."

"You're not very funny, Phil."

"Is that any better than intuition?"

"Let's not talk about it any more."

I agreed and we moved to less volatile subjects, and by the time we left the restaurant we were back where we started, which is to say I kissed her soundly, she went to do some shopping and I went back to the office, back to that old slave driver, Selma Livingston.

In the middle of the afternoon the bomb exploded.

Herb Lincoln called me up. He sounded very casual and he asked me if there was anything new and I told him about Anne's intuition and he laughed.

"Well," he said, "she may be right."

"Oh? What makes you think so?"

"Because it's happened to me now."

"You mean you've got it?" I could feel the cold sweat streaming from every pore.

"Had it since this morning," he said calmly. "Nothing to get excited about. I've called Lieutenant Grever, so he knows about it. It happened the way it did with Poley and Ernst. Only I'm not letting it get me down."

"How do you feel?"

"Fine. But I'm very much aware of the aura. You should have seen Sophie when I came out to get my breakfast. One look and you'd have thought I was Frankenstein's monster."

"Don't do anything rash, Herb, I'll be right over."

"No, Phil. I can work things out better by myself."

"But Herb—"

"No," he said harshly. "I've got to examine this whole thing clinically, logically."

"Don't let anything drive you to despair and destruction, Herb. Promise me that."

"Sophie said the same thing. She understands. Lord knows we've talked about it enough. But it is an odd thing. She says she feels like throwing things at me. And Jasper, poor kid, he doesn't know what's wrong. He took one look at me and let out a whoop you could have heard for a city block."

"What are you going to do, Herb?" The phone was slipping from my hand because of the sweat. I changed hands, rubbed my hand across my trousers to dry it, changed back.

"This calls for patience. Before we can move in a preventive direction, we have to know what it is and how it works. I have a little experiment to perform first to find out how far out this aura extends, what its hindering factors are, such as wood, steel, and so on. Routine things a researcher would do."

"How do you expect to carry them out?"

"Don't worry about it. I think I can handle it and I'll keep you informed."

"You say it started at breakfast, Herb. Maybe it's something in what you eat."

"No, it was before breakfast. I think it began as soon as I came out of the bathroom. Last night after talking with Lieutenant Grever I came home and I'd forgotten that I was supposed to take Sophie and Jasper out to dinner. We went out, came back put Jasper to bed. Then we stayed up all hours talking about it."

"Where's Sophie now—and Jasper?"

"They've gone to Santa Barbara. Sophie's mother lives there. She called a little while ago. It was the best way. It would be miserable for her being here."

"Herb, I'm coming over."

"No, you're not," he said emphatically. "This is a job for a man of science. There are certain logical steps to go through. You'd be in the way. Besides, you wouldn't be able to get near me. You'd either hate me or fear me. Lieutenant Grever understands. He wants me to let him know as soon as I determine the cause. I don't know how long it will take. A process of elimination, actually."

"Herb, for heaven's sake, is there anything I can do?"

"Not a thing, Phil. As I said, I'll keep in touch."

"Be careful, Herb. For God's sake be careful."

"I want to live as much you do, Phil. Don't worry."

Thirty hours later Dr. Herbert Lincoln was dead.

EIGHT

I didn't know of Herb's death until a half hour after it happened the following night. After his phone call I worked the rest of the afternoon, wondering if I ought to violate my agreement not to come to see him and do it anyway, and deciding not to, he was probably right. Selma making a wisecrack about my seeming to be preoccupied again.

When I got home I called Herb's apartment and it was a longtime before he answered. Then he said, "Oh, it's you, Phil. I wish you and the lieutenant would quit worrying. I'm still busy on it."

"Is it still with you?"

"Yes, it's still with me."

"Found out what it is yet?"

"No. Oh, it can't be neutralized, I found that out. I've tried just about everything. Soap, perfume, taking things orally. I've even tried the antidotes for nerve gas. Had some sent over."

"How do you know you've still got it?"

"There's a dog. Belongs to the people upstairs. They keep it in the back yard and when I go out there it starts yapping and snarling. That's how I know."

"How can you be sure? Do you know the dog?"

"It's a mangy old thing. Would hardly move a muscle at any other time. I know because I've even petted it. Besides, I met the woman downstairs. I was a good fifteen feet away, but she dropped the garbage she had brought out and ran back into the house. I don't know what she thinks; I don't much care. I do know it's a dreadful thing to have. I'm only glad she didn't clobber me with the garbage."

61

"You've got to find out what it is, Herb."

"You're telling me? I'll never get near another patient if I don't. But I'll get it. Whatever it is, the aura of hate and fear stays with me wherever I go, inside the house or not. I guess I must exude it—whether in the form of radiation or vapor or what I don't know just now. I know it's nothing in the house that acts continuously because it's just as strong outside. Personally, I favor the bacteria idea. But that's just a guess. Right now I'm going to have something to eat. Maybe the assimilation of food will reduce the effect. I'm not using anything from the refrigerator. I'm getting a meal sent up, leaving the door unlocked and putting the money on a card table. I'm hungry as hell, Phil."

"I'll bet you are. Why don't you let me bring you something?"

"No. I'll manage."

"I still don't like the thought of you——"

"Do you think I like it? Say, let me tell you something. One of our windows here was jimmied. Lieutenant Grever was going to send some men over, dust it for prints, but I told him to hold off until I satisfy myself on what this is. I think somebody came in last night when Sophie and Jasper and I were out to dinner, but whether that has anything to do with it, I'm not so sure. We checked and found nothing missing. It's odd, that's all."

"If somebody did plant something in your place, it knocks out the sunspots and little green men, doesn't it?"

"Unless the green men are handy with crowbars."

"Herb, I wish you weren't there by yourself."

"I'm glad I am. I couldn't think if somebody were here with me. Now listen, if anything happens, I'll let you know. Will you be home tonight?"

I told him I had a date with Anne, but that I'd stay home if he wanted me to.

"No, don't stay home. But maybe, just on the off-chance it means anything, lock up good. And don't call me when you get home. I may be asleep. Call me in the morning. I may know something then."

I went dancing with Anne, but I didn't have my heart in it. And as usual, I couldn't keep it from her.

"What's the matter, Phil?"

"Nothing," I said, knowing even as I said it, it was a losing battle.

"That's a lie," she said. "You were different at noon." She broke from me, took my arm. "Come on and sit down. You've got something to tell me."

As I've said, if it were anyone but Anne, I might have said nothing, but I couldn't hold out on her. I told her about it.

62

"And you're sitting there while Herb's so miserable in his apartment?" her eyes flashed. "I'm ashamed of you."

I almost laughed. Hysterically, that is. It took me the rest of the night to convince her Herb would be all right without me, but she insisted I call him on the way to taking her home. I did, and Herb was sore, said he'd been asleep.

It was only then that Anne would let me take her on home. Even when we parted I had the feeling she felt I ought to be doing something about it. I wished there were something I could do.

"You be careful yourself," was the last thing she said.

I was careful. I let myself into the apartment slowly. I turned on all the lights. I tried all the windows. Looked under everything. Nothing had been disturbed that I could see. Nothing had been added, nothing taken away.

I felt like a fool, slept like one.

I did my best work the next day, but I could tell by Selma's attitude I wasn't up to par. My mind was on Herb Lincoln. What was he doing? Why wouldn't he tell me? I called him several times during the day, but he was almost curt.

"I can tell you this," he said, "it's worse in the morning."

"Then whatever it is, it's stronger then."

"A brilliant deduction. Yes. Radiation, miasma, spray, sunspots, fog, aroma, vapor, ray, injection. Take your choice."

"I don't see why you don't get out of the house, Herb. Once out of there, maybe you'd get over it. Poley and Ernst stayed. Maybe that's where they made their big mistake."

"I've been over all that. I've even thought of asking you over to see if you'd get it just being here, but I decided against it because I don't think you would."

"I'd be willing, Herb."

"No. We might kill each other."

"Oh, come on, Herb."

"No, I mean it. This thing is dangerous when others are around. Look, you'd better call me later." He hung up.

I called him later. There was no answer. I called Lieutenant Grever. He said Herb had called him to tell him he was conducting an experiment and wouldn't be back for a while.

"He's a damn fool," Grever said, "leaving the house like that."

"That's Herb for you."

"He said he was taking his car. I hope he stays in it." As an afterthought he said, "With the windows rolled up."

I called several times, but still no answer. Just before I left to go home I called for the last time. Herb was there.

"Yes, I've made progress," he said. "I've even found out what it is." He sounded almost complacent about it.

"What is it?"

"It's a vapour, all right. It can be enclosed, however, in a room, or in a car. I found that out in a few elementary tests. As long as I was in the car I was all right, but I risked my life when I stepped out to perform my experiments. The vapor is really deadly to the carrier in the effect it has on others. I had no idea it was as bad as it is."

"Have you discovered what causes the vapor?"

"Yes, I have."

Pause. "Well, what is it?"

"I don't want to tell you right now, Phil. I've got to talk to Lieutenant Grever first. After that I'll tell you all about it when I see you. I just got in and I've got to do a little repairing. Besides, I'm hungry."

"You've got to do what?"

"Repairing. You see, I ran into a little trouble. Nothing that a little merthiolate and bandages won't fix up. Need a bath, too."

I didn't like his reticence about telling me, but he was right. Grever ought to know first. "What can I do, Herb?"

"Nothing, really. I've got to run out to the hospital lab after a bit. I want to find out what the stuff's made of. Once I find out, maybe I can work on an antidote. We all ought to have an antidote handy. The stuff's powerful, as I've said." He paused for a moment. "I can tell you this much, Phil. I think it works through the enzymes, through the sweat glands, is absorbed by the body which manufactures the secretion. It's damned interesting."

"I still would like to do something to help."

"You can help by just sitting tight. I'll have the answer pretty soon. I know enough now not to get exposed again, so I'll probably be all right in the morning. I'll talk to you then."

"Herb, listen——"

"I've got to rush, Phil. I've got to call Grever and then get to the hospital. Call Grever if you want. See you."

I went home, but all I could think of was Herb. Anne called and we went out to dinner. Of course I told her what was on my mind and then there were two of us sitting like zombies, hoping Herb knew what he was doing, until I couldn't stand it any more.

"Let's go to the hospital," I said. "I don't feel like sitting around here thinking. Maybe we won't get into the lab where he'll be working, but at least we can talk to him through the door or the intercom or something."

Anne nodded, her eyes wide. "I've got a feeling," she said. "And I don't like it."

"What's the feeling?" And before she said it I could feel it too.

Call it a presentiment, a psychic warning. She called it intuition.

"Something's wrong."

We got out of there fast and headed for the hospital. Herb wasn't there. A technician named Maria Morrisey said she'd been waiting for him for over an hour, had everything out, ready for him just as he'd asked, did we by any chance know where he was?

We left the hospital, hurried to his apartment. Herb wasn't there either. We rang the bell. No sign of life.

"Oh, Phil!" Anne cried. "Herb's in trouble!"

"I hope that's not an understatement."

The nearest phone was in a drugstore two blocks away. I called Lieutenant Grever.

"Dr. Lincoln is dead," he said simply. "He was killed by a man named Homer Petry over an hour ago while he was on his way to the hospital. You'd better come on down."

I almost staggered out of the phone booth. I know I wasn't steady, my feet were like lead weights, and all I could see was Herb's cold, professional, determined face before me. I didn't have to tell Anne, but I mumbled what I could of it to her as we walked from the drugstore. Saying it made it seem even worse, and by the time we got to the car my feet were numb and I felt the numbness crawling up. I fought for control. My God, I thought, Herb's gone. Herb's gone. Herb's gone. And I dropped my head back on the seat. Everything was closing in, we were all doomed, we'd go one by one, and it was only a matter of time before we'd all be gone.

"Phil," Anne said, shaking me, "now's not the time to go to pieces."

I'd forgotten she was there beside me in the car. I'd even forgotten we were in a car. I raised my head. I saw the cars going by, I saw the bright drugstore. Anne was right. This wasn't the time to go to pieces. What had happened to me?

"I'm sorry," I said. "It just got me, that's all."

"I know."

"Three of us gone."

"Don't think about it."

"No," I said, beginning to revive, "now's the time to think about it. Four of us left. We've got to keep us alive."

"You need a drink." Anne seldom suggested anything like that. I knew then how far I must have gone.

"No, Anne, I don't need a drink." I sat up. "What I've got to do is go down and see Lieutenant Grever."

I told Anne I'd get her a cab, but of course it was like talking to my right arm which had no intention of being separated from the rest of me. So Anne came along.

Lieutenant Grever was badly shaken, I could see that. Almost as badly shaken as I. His eyes were deeply troubled, his lips grim. I introduced Anne. He merely nodded to her.

"It's all my fault," he said when we were closeted with him in the same room in which Herb and I had talked with him before. "I told him to be careful, I told him not to try anything on his own, but he was so set on it he wouldn't listen to me. I should have sent somebody over there." He turned to me. "He seemed so damned sure of himself."

"Herb was like that," I said. "How did it happen?"

"He started out in his car for the hospital, which in itself was bad enough—even though he'd made a little foray in it in the afternoon for some crazy experiment. I never did find out what that was all about. Anyway, he was so occupied with this thing he forgot to look at the gas gauge. He ran out of gas. So what did he do? He got out and started walking the rest of the way to the hospital, the most idiotic thing he could have done! He signed his death warrant the moment he did that."

"But he did get out of the car this afternoon?"

"Yes. He was going to tell me all about it after he got to the hospital. For a man as logical as Dr. Lincoln, it was a foolhardy thing to tempt fate a second time the way he did."

"He thought people would run away from him, is that it? He forgot about the other reaction, the one of hate."

Grever nodded. "That's about it. That's what killed him. Hate and wine and Homer Petry."

Anne said, "Who is Homer Petry?"

"A wino. We've got a million of them here in L.A. Homer's ordinarily harmless—oh, he's done his share of muggings, don't think he hasn't, but that's in what the Department considers Homer's past. He's getting on in years, Homer is, and he's not been in trouble for some time."

"Where did it happen?" I asked.

"About three blocks from the hospital. Homer was sitting with three buddies on the steps of the flophouse that's been his home for the past ten years. Dr. Lincoln had to walk down that street. Homer says he saw him, says he appeared to be deep in thought, his eyes on the sidewalk, a package under his arm. He was walking fast. When Dr. Lincoln came close to the steps, Homer's friends commenced trembling. He says he didn't get it at first and wondered why. They'd been drinking sherry all day and they shouldn't have been acting that way.

"Then Homer says it hit him. It just came over him like—well,

66

to use Homer's expression, he said he knows now how a bull feels when he sees red. He was sitting there with the bottle one minute and the next thing he knew Dr. Lincoln was an object of intense hatred. Everything Homer had hated in his life became lodged for that moment in Dr. Lincoln. He rushed down the steps and commenced hitting the doctor with the wine bottle."

Lieutenant Grever shook his head. "One blow—the first blow—probably would have killed him. But Homer was out of his mind. Even when Dr. Lincoln was down he kept hitting him." Grever glanced at Anne, then at me, his eyes curiously bright. "There isn't much left of Dr. Lincoln's face."

Anne shuddered, turned away.

"I'm sorry," the lieutenant said.

I said, "Herb was married . . ."

"I called his wife."

"Poor Sophie," Anne said.

"Homer's in the hospital," Grever said. "He's convinced he's losing his mind, swears he'll never touch a drop of wine again. It's a confusing thing. I know he didn't mean to do it, but from our standpoint there's nothing we can do but hold him for it, charge him with it." He added grimly, "I just don't want it to happen again."

"You said Dr. Lincoln was carrying a package under his arm, Lieutenant. Do you have it?"

"No, Mr. DeMoss, I don't. Whatever happened to it, I don't know. There was glass all around—mostly the wine bottle—but it may be some of the shards we found come from another container. We're trying to find out if they do. But what good it will do us when we find out, I can only guess. We're also making a close search of the area. It could be that the package went sailing off somewhere, under steps or across the street, or that somebody picked it up—in which case we might find out another way, if you follow me."

"I follow you, and I'm sorry for the man who did, if it's true."

Lieutenant Grever sighed. "I wanted you down here because you worked with Dr. Lincoln on it."

"A rather ironic way of putting it. Herb was always a pretty closemouthed fellow. He told me he was going to clear it all with you before he said anything to me. The way he talked, he had it pretty well tied up."

"I'm sorry to hear that. And to think this had to happen because of the lack of a little gasoline."

"For want of a nail . . ." Anne said.

"Yes." The lieutenant lit a cigarette, exhaled a plume of smoke at the room's only light in the ceiling. "Mr. DeMoss, I want a

67

meeting to be held of the surviving members of the Forty-two Club."

I said I'd be glad to get them together, when did he want to have me do it.

"Right now." He looked at his wrist watch. "I suggest you start calling them at once. Tell them it's a matter of life and death. Insist that they drop everything and meet you and someone from the police department at your place at once."

"Two live in San Benuto. It'll take a little time."

"I don't care how long it takes, I don't care where they live. We've got to get to them as quickly as possible before somebody else turns up dead." He smiled thinly. "I've had a look at you, Mr. DeMoss. Now I want to have look at the others."

NINE

It was nearly midnight before I got them all together in my apartment, the Klocks, Clifford Ellis and Jake Hardy. Lieutenant Grever could have done it in an hour, but he said he didn't want it to look like a police move and he was reluctant to use coercion.

"They'll come," he said. "They value their lives. They're curious, too. Anybody doesn't come, then I'll start wheels rolling."

It was eleven o'clock before a telephone operator in San Benuto located Jake Hardy, and I had a tough time convincing him he ought to come down because he evidently was out on the town with some friends, but he finally agreed. I hoped the edge would wear off before he arrived. Clifford Ellis wasn't home, but I learned from his housekeeper that he was spending the night in Los Angeles. A little more prodding and I got the name Philomena Wren. It was an unusual name, and here Grever lent a hand. His men ran down a Philomena Wren, a minor television actress, in an apartment in the valley, and there we located Elliis. He treated my invitation as a big joke, but he did promise to come, although it took him over an hour to make it. The Klocks were easiest. They were home watching television, and they arrived first. They knew about Herb Lincoln. They'd watched a news program.

Glenn Klock was pale, nervous and dazed as I made the introduction to Grever and handed him a drink. He just stared at Grever, standing in the middle of my living room, the glass in his hand. Lula gave the lieutenant a glance and then moved to the davenport to sit beside Anne, her eyes shifting fearfully to me. I asked her if she wanted a drink.

"No, Phil," Lula said in a voice I had to strain to hear, "I want to keep a clear head." She looked worriedly at Glenn who was still staring at Grever. I'd never seen Lula like this. Ordinarily she's on her feet moving about or talking animatedly to someone about anything from Byzantine art to cell differentiation, and frenetically tossing down refreshment in the process.

"Where is it all going to end?" Glenn had turned and said this to me in a loud voice. Mostly, Glenn's soft-spoken. "Now it's Herb Lincoln." Even louder: "Who's the crazy man, Phil? Why are we being picked on?"

Grever, who had been watching him from my armchair, said quietly, "Who says it's a man, Mr. Klock? And who says your group is being picked on?"

Glenn turned to him again. With control he said more calmly, "I—I think that's rather obvious, isn't it?"

"No," said Grever flatly.

"I've been worried about Glenn," Lula said. "I want him to stay home until all this is over, but he won't do it."

"That's ridiculous, Lula," Glenn said, "and you know it."

"It's not ridiculous. You'll end up just like Ernst and Poley and now Herb."

"But, Lula, they got it even though they stayed home."

Grever said, "Mrs. Klock, you're pretty worried, aren't you?"

"Yes, I am. I can't even go to my classes. I can't even study. I keep thinking, wondering . . ." She actually shuddered, I saw the beginnings of tears in her eyes, and Glenn moved to the davenport to sit beside her, taking her hand.

"You worry too much," he said. "You worry enough for half-a-dozen people."

She said ruefully, "You should have graduated in the class of nineteen forty-three."

Glenn smiled. "I'm for that. Maybe even forty-one."

"Anything but this crazy class."

Grever leaned forward in his chair. "Mr. DeMoss says you're a researcher for an encyclopedia firm, Mr. Klock."

"Yes, I am. North American Encyclopedia."

"Just what do you do?"

"Oh, I assign research projects in various subjects—you've seen the articles signed with the name or names of the contributors. Some of the smaller subjects I do myself." He blinked his eyes at Grever. "Is there a reason for your wanting to know?"

"Yes. I wondered if your research took you by any chance into the fields of psychology and kindred sciences." Lieutenant Grever, I decided, was neither stupid nor dishonest. I was getting to like him.

Glenn's eyes didn't falter as he said, "Of course, that's what you're here for, to try to dig something out of us about the deaths. Well, I've done a little work in the lines you speak of, but nothing of a laboratory nature. Nothing but paper work." He managed a thin smile. "I hope that doesn't disappoint you."

"Who did your article on nerve gas or G-gas?"

"I don't recall that we have an article on either. I think the subject is included under the general titles of gases in warfare and chemical warfare."

"And who did those?"

"I don't recall. Sometimes the service chief—a general, for example—may assign a number of people in a branch or the specific unit itself to prepare something for us. We don't use all of it and of course we don't get all of it either because of the restricted nature of some of these things. Sometimes we assign a college specialist or a pure research worker in the field."

"I see."

Lula said, "Glenn's job is a frustrating one, Lieutenant Grever. He does so want to have specific information, but sometimes he just can't——"

"Let me tell him, honey," Glenn said, smiling, patting her head. "What Lula means is I'm too much of a perfectionist. It gets me down sometimes that I can't do everything myself. But there happen to be other people on the staff."

Grever said, "You've done no research yourself?"

"Research?" Glenn goggled at him. "That's my job."

"I mean laboratory research—actually work with chemicals."

"No. I think I've already said that. But I won't deny that sometimes I wish I did. It's no secret I have considered a career in chemistry in college—I have a B.S. and a Masters—but encyclopedia work seemed to present so many challenges and——"

"Would you call yourself a frustrated chemist?"

"Well, I wouldn't go so far as to say that. I'm as much a frustrated mathematician or physicist as I am a frustrated chemist—or even electronics engineer now that the space age is with us. But I make a good living and I guess I'll stick with it."

There was a moment's pause, and into the breach Lula inserted these quiet words: "Is it that you think Glenn really had anything to do with the deaths, Lieutenant? Is that why you're asking these questions?"

"I don't know what to think, Mrs. Klock," Grever said honestly. "Three men are dead. I think they were killed by something. I want to know what, how, why and by whom, if a person is involved. The more information I have, the better I will be able to decide what to do. As the wife of a researcher, you must bow to the logic of that."

"I suppose so," Lula said. "But Glenn had nothing to do with it. I can tell you that."

"She's right," Glenn said. "I simply wouldn't have the time."

"Let us hope," Grever said, "that that is so."

It wasn't long after this that Cliff Ellis arrived carrying with him his usual shoulder chip, saying, "Well, well, look who's all here," as he handed me his coat. "Looks like Old Home Week on a reduced scale." He grinned at me. "Thought we'd better have another meeting while we still had a quorum, is that it, Phil?"

"It's no joke, Cliff," I said. Then I introduced him to Lieutenant Grever.

Cliff flashed his grin at him, extended his hand. "Glad you could make it, Lieutenant." He turned to me. "You didn't say any police brass would be here. All I expected was a plain old patrolman, or, at the very most, a sergeant."

I said, "You may be glad Lieutenant Grever's in charge before you're through, Cliff."

Grever said, "You did understand about Dr. Lincoln, didn't you, Mr. Ellis?"

"Understand about him?"

"That he's dead."

"Of course."

"You don't seem very upset."

"I do not quarrel with destiny, Lieutenant. Whatever the bright ironic gods decide is inexorable. All the tears in the world will fail to cancel out what has been written. I hope I don't sound too Far Eastern." He chuckled and found a chair. "How are you Anne, Lula?"

"I'm afraid I don't find you very funny at the moment," Anne said coldly.

Lula said, "You make it more difficult every day for me to like you, Cliff."

Cliff said soberly, "The natural habitat of us Ellises."

"Stop play-acting," Glenn said. "Lieutenant, Cliff always tries out his lines before he writes them. Spouts his books—or somebody else's—all the time. He's not really like this."

"That's right," Cliff said. "I'm perfectly harmless." His eyes went from one to the other of us. "May I ask what would be served by saying how I feel about what has happened? If you must know, there were times when I felt Herb Lincoln was too dedicated a man—dedicated to Herb Lincoln, that is. Then there are times when I wonder if this is either a disadvantage or unwise. Was it wrong for Herb's heart to be in the form of a caduceus,

71

beating more for the profession than it did for humanity? Then I look at myself and say even worse things about me." I put a drink in his hand at this moment and he looked down at it. "I'll miss him, don't think I won't, if that is what is expected of me to say. For all his faults, I'll miss him like hell." He took a long drink while the rest of us sat there and looked at him. I had never known him to drop the cynicism he wore like armor, and I wondered if I were seeing him as he really was.

Grever broke the silence by saying, "I understand, Mr. Ellis, that you feel people would be better off dead."

Cliff looked up bright-eyed, the old Cliff again. "Now where in the world would you hear a thing like that?"

"Is it true?"

"Is death preferable to life? It seems to me a moot question, particularly since the world is having to choose between a slow death by radiation and a quick one by atomic blast."

"A few years ago, perhaps. Now there seems to be some hope for humanity."

"There was never much hope, Lieutenant."

Lieutenant Grever said gruffly, "It seems to me you never got over your college bull-session days."

"That is the only time of honesty in our lives before embracing the insanity of adulthood."

"Are you a beatnik, Mr. Ellis?"

"I am not a policeman, Mr. Grever."

Glenn said, "Cut it out, Cliff. Everybody knows you're an intellectual. We all accept it. Now let's get on with it."

Cliff smiled. "On the contrary, Glenn. Lieutenant Grever didn't know. Now he knows I'm a breaker of idols. Don't you, Lieutenant?"

Grever shrugged. "A nihilist, a negativistic thinker, perhaps. Or so you would have me believe. A pity you never thought of a law enforcement career. You might have levelled off." I admired Grever's control. He continued to sit in his chair, the picture of a relaxed man. But his eyes didn't look tired any more. They were bright blue and they dwelt on Clifford Ellis. "I could have taught you a lot if they had assigned you to me."

Now Cliff laughed. "You should have taken up a literary career, Lieutenant. You're halfway there already."

Just then the doorbell rang again and I went to admit Jake Hardy. He came in red-faced, blustering and angry, taking off his coat. The gum he was chewing failed to disguise his beer-and-whisky breath. "What's it all about, Phil, that stuff about Herb?" His speech was slurred. He turned to those in the room.

72

"You've got a radio in your car," Cliff said. "Don't you ever listen to it?"

"No, I didn't."

"Well, the doctor isn't with us any more."

"I'll be damned," Jake said, walking into the room. "They got Herb Lincoln, huh?" His head was bobbing a little as he looked around. His eyes stopped at Grever and he stared at him, his jaws working on his gum.

"I'm Lieutenant Grever," the policeman said, getting up. "You must be Jake Hardy."

"Yeah, yeah." His eyes were dazed and they made a circuit of the room again. "Jesus, only four of us left."

"The last of the ten little Indians," Cliff said.

Jake turned woebegone eyes to me. "Need a drink, Prez," he said. "Make it a double. God knows I need it." He dropped into the only empty chair in the room.

"The question before us," Cliff said, "is who's next. Just filling you in, Jake. Before you rang the bell, I nominated Lieutenant Grever. What do you think of that?"

Jake stared at him. He didn't seem to understand. I had never seen him this way. The combination of drink and the verification of Herb's death seemed too much for him. Jake had always been a jokester, a life-of-the-party type. Now he looked like an old man, the beginning of rheumy eyes, flushed vein-marked face. Of course he was older than the rest of us. Nearing forty-five, anyway.

"You've had a few," Cliff said.

Jake sighed wearily. "Yeah, I have." He made an effort to collect himself. "You were nominating?"

"Yes," Cliff said. "Do you want to run?"

"Cut it out!" Glenn said angrily. "You'd think nothing was happening."

Cliff's eyes swung around to Glenn and impaled him. "Must you always take things so seriously, Glenn? This isn't an encyclopedia we're compiling here. We can afford to be human."

I decided to break it up. "Look, we can insult each other any old time. Right now we've got more important things to do."

"Like what?" Cliff asked.

"Like making sure we're all around next year at this time."

"You think we won't be?" Jake wanted to know.

"We all face danger," I said. "I want you to hear about it."

"If we're in some kind of danger," Jake said, "I want to hear about it."

"Oh, we're in danger, all right," Cliff said. "Obesity, atrophy and greed. That's three good dangers. We face them all. We can take them up one by one, starting with obesity."

"Cliff," I said, "will you kindly shut up?"

"Not kindly. I forgot you're the president."

I gave him a withering glance and went on, "Now, we're all familiar with what happened to Poley and Ernst. What you haven't heard is that the same thing happened to Herb."

Cliff looked at me blankly. "Quit the kidding, Phil. He was clubbed to death by a wino named Peters or something. Hell, you told me so yourself."

"So I did. What I didn't tell you is he contracted the same thing—call it a disease for the lack of a better name for it—as Poley and Ernst. He was trying to work out what it was when he was killed."

Jake shook his head. "I don't get it."

"Why, Jake?"

"You say he had the same thing but he didn't kill himself?"

Lieutenant Grever said, "That's right, Mr. Hardy. He was driving his car to the hospital, he ran out of gas, had to get out of the car, and was killed. He was on his way to analyze the substance he attributed his condition to."

Glenn rubbed his forehead. "I'm afraid I don't get it either. Phil, when you called me on the phone yesterday you said this thing makes people afraid of you or hate you. You didn't say anything about people wanting to kill you."

I told them then how it was a deadly two-edged thing, and that the fear was more terror, that the hate was murderous. I told them how Terry McGowan had attacked his father, how somebody must have attacked Herb when he got out of his car to conduct the experiment we were never to hear about.

"Herb said it was an aura—an aura of fear and hate—and we can only imagine which emotion would be engendered in the living thing that came within that aura. He said it was a vapor thrown off by the body—a nerve gas that induced these reactions."

"In a way," Grever said, "it is like a drug, a narcotic. A narcotic doesn't affect everyone the same way. It seems to depend upon the basic structure of the subject's personality. It makes wild men of some, sleepers of others."

Then everybody was talking at once, and we got into the meat of it. Grever was good. He was watchful and alert, yet he managed to question everyone without making it appear planned and deliberate. I served more drinks and everybody loosened up, Lula taking off her shoes, Jake losing his dazed look, and Cliff becoming more human.

"O.K., so what are we supposed to do?" Jake asked at one point. "Now we know about it. How do we protect ourselves from this—this plague?"

Grever admitted he didn't know. "All I can say is being fore-warned is being forearmed. Now that you know the face of the enemy, the idea is not to panic. If it happens to you, let the others know, call me, but for God's sake, stay home. You are safe inside your own home. The vapor can be confined. I'll get somebody on the job who knows something about such things, and we'll work something out."

Jake shook his head. For some reason the drinks had revived him. "It just doesn't make sense that anybody'd do this to a group like the Forty-two Club."

"Things like this never make sense," Grever said.

Cliff said soberly, "It would make sense if we knew. Every-thing makes sense when you know. Even life."

I said we didn't know for sure that the Forty-two Club was marked for extinction, that all we could do was assume it was.

"It's safer, assuming that," Glenn said.

"I've thought it was all along," Lula said. "I thought so when Poley and Ernst were gone."

"I don't need to get it," Cliff said with a wry chuckle. "People hate me anyway."

"Yes," Glenn said pleasantly. "In your case it would be wasted effort."

"Touché," Cliff said. "Do you suppose it was congenital, this aura I seem to have around me?"

That set us off again, exploring what was known about the gas or whatever it was, for what distance it was effective, rehash-ing what Ellen McGowan and Rose Mollinauer had said about it, assuming that it could not penetrate a closed door, that it came and went (as in Poley's case) for no apparent reason.

"Since Herb said he had a 'substance,' the trigger must be something three-dimensional," Glenn said. "I mean that as op-posed to sunspots or inducing waves from a distant star."

"Whatever it was, Herb thought it could be analyzed," I said.

"Something from the refrigerator," Lula suggested. "Isn't there a gas in refrigerator coils?"

"It only attacks men," Cliff said. "That seems unfair."

It was after one o'clock when the gathering broke up, and when they were gone, Grever, Anne and I sat looking gloomily at each other. It hadn't gone too well, we hadn't covered the ground we'd set out to, and it seemed ridiculous to think that any of the people who'd been there could be guilty of wanting to do away with the others.

"I tell you, I don't know what to think," Grever said, his face a dark study. "That Ellis isn't a very pleasant man, but as you've said, I don't think he'd move himself to do a thing like this."

Anne said, "It seems to me Clifford Ellis enjoys being an iconoclast. To him the worst thing in the world is sentiment—publicly. Privately I think he really feels things. I can't see him doing it either."

"Well, that leaves Glenn Klock and Jake Hardy," I said.

"Mr. Klock hardly seems the type, and Mr. Hardy doesn't have the ability." Grever screwed up his mouth. "Even so, if I were forced to guess, my guess would be Mr. Hardy. Why does the man drink so much? There must be a reason."

"Oh, there's Lula," Anne said. "She resents those in the group who were married and had families."

"Is that true?"

"No, Lieutenant. Anne's just ribbing me. The other day I was just stating a hypothetical thing to her, trying to show how you could establish a motive if you tried hard enough, twisted the facts around enough. I really don't think Lula resented Poley or Ernst or Herb."

"She seemed rather disturbed. There's nothing that says it can't be a woman, if it is anyone at all."

Anne said brightly, "Well, there's always me."

"Uh-huh," I said. "You met them for the first time the night of the dinner. So you've built up motives galore."

"If it *is* me," Anne said, "I'm saving you to the last."

"Why prolong the agony?"

"I'm saving you because I want you all to myself. Don't want to share you with anyone. Isn't that motive enough?"

Grever shot me a glance. "That's right. There's always Philip DeMoss."

"Let's hope there always will be," I said.

"Are you planning it that way?"

"Are you serious, Lieutenant?"

"Maybe. Just playing all the angles." He smiled at Anne. "Can I drop you somewhere now that I've alienated you and your husband-to-be?"

Once again I had my nightcap, sat around thinking for another hour. But, as usual, I got no place. Except to bed. I should have stayed in bed the next day.

It was the most horrible day in my life.

TEN

The most terrible day of my life started out with deceptive innocence. I slept later than I intended, for one thing, which gave it immediately the feeling of normality. And then, when a glance at the clock told me I could not possibly sleep another minute, I marshalled what little will power I'm able to muster at that hour, and crawled out of bed. This is always the low point of the day with me, a time when I'm torn between sneaking back to bed (and saying to hell with the world) and rallying my forces to make a frontal attack on the day. Of course I always come through, the combative part of me inevitably dispelling thoughts of the deliciousness of continued sleep. On this day I thought: Some day, Philip DeMoss, you'll be able to thumb your nose at life's demands and go back to bed, but you'll never be able to do it unless you get on the ball now. And then I thought: But don't you say this to yourself every day?

It was true, I reflected sadly. But by that time I was halfway roused, and events of the preceding night were beginning to filter past the shreds of sleep, and I knew I was awake for good.

At once, while I went through the automatic motions of getting dressed, shaving, selecting what I was going to wear, which required no thought, I found myself recalling bits of last night's conversation, interspersing these recollections with guilt feelings about the office. Selma would never forgive me if I didn't offer more than token loyalty to it. In fact, I wouldn't even forgive myself. But if there was to be an answer to the untimely deaths, somebody was going to have to think about it. Not just Lieutenant Grever. Having made that rationalization, I could further enjoy thinking about Jake Hardy (Grever leaned toward him as the guilty man), the Klocks (sure Glenn was quiet and subdued, but hadn't Grever himself said you have to look out for the studious type?), and Clifford Ellis (how sarcastic can you get and still keep your friends?). To say nothing of Lula (maybe she did have a motive) and Anne (no, absolutely not, it couldn't be Anne). But what about Mrs. Mollinauer, Mrs. Poley, Mrs. Lincoln? We'd overlooked them. They could be as guilty as Lula, for example, couldn't they?

I laughed at myself. Suppose a man is killed by a tiny meteor fragment. It comes barrelling down out of the sky, strikes him down as he walks by the side of the road, makes a hole clean through him. The man staggers on for a half-block, say. Maybe even crawls a little way before he dies. The police are aroused. The hole through this man—we'll call him Joe Smith—is just about the size of a .38 bullet. It could be an unsolved murder. Maybe somebody might even be executed for it, some guy who happened to be nearby and who fired his gun at something a few hours before—a rat, say.

And all the time it would be a little meteorite that did the dirty work.

"Isn't that about as fantastic as this?" I said to myself.

"Unbelievable," I answered.

"Maybe." Then I thought: Meteor fragments have been known to come to earth. I remembered seeing a picture of an automobile radiator with a .38 hole in it. Actually, the .38 caliber meteor fragment was still stuck under the hood in the exhaust manifold. At least so said the newspicture outlines.

It could be, I told myself, that we're trying to pin something on somebody when there's nothing to pin. But Herb said before he died that he'd found out what it was. But did he say who he thought was guilty? No, he said nothing about anybody being guilty. He was too interested in the scientific aspects of the thing. Was that it? Was it just a meteor fragment?

Easy, I told myself, glancing at my dresser clock as I tied my tie. Next thing you know you'll be back to the little green monsters and ray guns and heaven knows what else. Forget about meteor fragments.

I'd been so occupied I saw now there wasn't time to prepare any kind of breakfast. I would have to grab something downtown. I put on my suitcoat, let myself out the back door and went down to my car. Even as I entered the garage I found myself glancing at the radiator of my Chevvy. No sign of any .38 caliber meteor fragment. For some reason I felt better about things. I got in the car and soon became part of streaming Los Angeles traffic.

Because I had left my apartment a little ahead of the usual time (no breakfast), there were few cars in the parking lot a block away from my office, and I managed to take one of the spaces near the rear (less wear and tear on bumpers to the rear). I was feeling good. I ought to come down a little early every day, avoid the rush, I told myself (I'd done this before). Even Gus, the lot attendant, wasn't in sight. Probably getting coffee somewhere. Well, he knew my car, so that was no problem.

I stepped out to the sidewalk, hurried to Sally's Copper Kettle. Nobody named Sally anything ran Sally's Copper Kettle, and where they got the name I don't know because there was no copper kettle in sight. Not even the picture of one. The short-order joint was run by a man named Larry Mason and the

78

joke was his brother was Perry Mason, except the joke wasn't funny to Larry. But Larry could do good things to eggs, if not to much of anything else.

It was pleasant to walk into the place, see it wasn't crowded. It was fine to anticipate Larry's coffee and a leisurely breakfast of scrambled eggs. Or maybe two eggs straight up with a side order of crisp bacon. It was good to be alive. Meteor fragments and fear and death were far away.

But no sooner had I walked in, letting the door close behind me, than the three people in the place—two burly men on stools at the counter and Larry himself in front of the shiny silver coffee urns—turned to me as one man.

I never saw such fear on the face of a human being as I saw on Larry's face. There was no recognition in his eyes. He dropped the cup and saucer he was holding. He stared at me. His face was white.

One of the two husky men at the counter rose. Larry's face had been fearful. This man's face was outraged. He was still chewing his food, but his eyes were slitted in hate, and he walked toward me with the easy walk of a fighter, his arms hanging loose at his sides.

I would have stayed to see how it came out if alarm bells hadn't started clanging with terrible jackhammer rapidity in my head.

I had it.

Whatever it was, *I had it*.

First Poley, then Ernst, then Herb.

Now *me*.

Yes, now a lawyer named Philip DeMoss, a nice young man who usually minded his own business.

Judging by the looks of the big man coming toward me, I wouldn't have it long. I'd be dead before I experienced much of it.

Of course I got out of there. I opened the door, stepped out and closed the door behind me. Then I commenced walking down the sunlit Los Angeles street. Not too fast. Lightly on my feet. I was waiting to hear Sally's Copper Kettle's door open. When it opened I would start running. I was conserving my wind. But it never did open.

My mind was racing frantically and getting nowhere. I had to get home. Lieutenant Grever had said to stay home, he'd get somebody out to the house, guard the place, send somebody out to study the thing. Somebody who specialized in things like this, he said. But I had left my house. What to do now? Go home, you fool, I told myself.

Still churning violently, my brain cried out that I ought to get in touch with Grever first. Sure, sure, I ought to get in touch. But how? I can't walk to the police station. Somebody might get put out on the way and hit me with a wine bottle. And at the police station I would get no better treatment than I would from Larry Mason, who knew me. If Poley's wife couldn't stand him, how could I expect anbody who didn't know me to show me any consideration?

Get your car. Yes, that was it. I'd parked the car. I'd get it, run out to the apartment and stay there. Maybe I could do what Herb did, start a logical study of the thing, decide what it was. If Herb could do it, why couldn't I?

I went around the block. Several times I came upon people who reacted violently when I got close to them. One young woman, obviously a secretary or stenographer, a fine young lady, walking fast in my direction, stopped before me, her eyes widening. She swallowed hard, staring at me, then opened her mouth, put her fist to her cheeks and let go with one of the most blood-curdling shrieks I've ever heard.

I ran, echoes of the scream ringing in my ears. Broad daylight in busy Los Angeles. A running man. A screaming girl. Did I say I ran? I practically flew. If I stopped, if too many people got in my way, I didn't know how it would turn out. Or let's say I did know how it would turn out but I didn't want to think about it.

There was a passageway off the avenue, a paved area between two buildings. I ducked in there, ran down its full length, came to an area behind these buildings where I caught my breath. No one was here, so I managed to rest for a while. I heard no sirens, no great commotion. Nobody had come down the passageway after me.

I realized I was lucky. I also realized I'd have to watch my step if I was going to get to my car. A few more shrieking young women and I'd have had it.

When my wind came back I tried to figure out where the parking lot was. It should have been where the buildings behind me were. But the structures were far too solid to be any part of a parking lot. They were rears of stores. I decided I'd proceed down the alleyway in the same direction that I had started down the street to my left. I walked gingerly. I was hungry. My nerves were on edge. I didn't know when I'd run into the next person, and then whether he or she would fear or hate me made it that much more uncertain.

I was within a hundred feet of the end of the alley. I could see cars going by in the street beyond. Since the cars were going in only one direction I assumed it was a one-way street. For the life of me I couldn't decide what street it was.

It was then I saw the dog, or the dog saw me. Anyway, it was passing the alley, sensed my presence and stopped at the entrance to it. Then I heard it growl and it started for me as fast as it could come, a yellow-and-white mongrel, angry-eyed, teeth bared, growling as it came.

I turned and ran, but it was on me before I got very far, nipping my buttocks, tearing my trousers. It had come so fast that it bounced off me, spun around on the ground and started for me again in a frency of pumping legs, teeth, wild eyes and snarls. It hit my pants legs, commenced clawing at me, its jaws snapping. I didn't just stand there; I looked around, spied a door and stumbled toward it, the dog still at my leg. I opened the door, squeezed it shut behind me, the dog's snoot caught there because it still had hold of my trousers leg. It was no time for niceties. I kicked at the dog's jaw with my unencumbered foot, yanked mightily on the door, heard the dog's yelp of pain and frustration.

The door closed. I breathed a sigh of relief, my heart pounding. A hasty inspection showed a frayed trouser cuff, a part of the seat of my pants missing, but no blood. I was glad of that. I turned around. Stairs.

I went up them. I could not go out the door I'd come in; the dog might still be there. Where was the parking lot? Where was I going? What would happen if I ran into someone now?

The upstairs corridor went forward. I followed it. It made an abrupt turn to the right. I went with it, passing doors, another stairway up. What I wanted was a stairway down.

A door opened. A pasty-faced blonde took one look at me as she started out, and started screaming. We stood there for a moment, the girl screaming and I staring. There seemed nothing else to do but run, but some calculation inside me told me I'd run into nothing but trouble if I left her there, so I—believe me it was purely reflex action—let go with a fist in her face. Her face registered astonishment at first, then bewilderment. Finally, her eyes rolled up inside her head and she slumped to the floor.

Her feet stuck out into the corridor. I lifted them into the air, reached over, drew the door shut as I dropped the feet.

I heard steps on the stairs, a commotion somewhere in the building. The blonde had had a good pair of lungs; her screams were beginning to pay off. I remembered the stairs going up, so I ran back to where they were and started up them. Now I was on the third floor. I ran down a corridor similar to the one beneath me, but when I turned the corner I saw windows on my right. They opened out to nothing—at least it seemed like nothing at first, until I looked more closely and saw the roof of the building next door. Since there were no stairs at the end of the corridor, I unlatched the nearest window, raised it, and dropped to the roof.

I felt like a fleeing criminal. I shouldn't have hit the blonde. That was a mistake, my legal mind informed me. And I agreed. It was self-defence, though, wasn't it? But I couldn't stop to think of the problem past, my problem was what to do now and I didn't know which way to go. I went to the front of the building, looked down on leisurely traffic and a normal-looking world. I didn't want to go to the rear. The dog might still be in the alley, pawing at that door I'd closed. But it was a good twenty feet to the street here at the front.

There was a square cover in the roof, raised from the roof proper. I went over to it, tried to raise it. It moved, but it wouldn't come up. Just then I heard a yell, saw a man in suspenders and undershirt in the window I'd just crawled through. Behind him was the blonde, pointing at me with a trembling finger. I gave a mighty yank at the cover. There was the sound of splitting wood. Then it came up.

Below me was a wooden ladder. I eased myself down from the roof, clambered down the ladder wondering what now, Philip DeMoss, where's that parking lot? A door at my elbow opened. The face of a man appeared there. I could tell by the look in his eyes he was scared to death of me and I was glad he was because that made two of us. He slammed the door and I started down this passageway, found stairs, ran down them to the street. Cars were moving by swiftly, faster than they had looked from the roof. The sun was shining, nobody was on the street. I stepped out and started to walk. No casual stroller, I. I wanted that parking lot and I wanted it bad. But where was it? I tried to reconstruct my actions, tried to determine which street this was. How confused can a person get once he gets off an old, familiar street?

Dogs. I kept an eye out for them. I passed stores. Plumbing fixtures. Wholesale candies. I was thankful everybody seemed busy. Too busy to be walking on a glorious morning like this.

A man was washing the windows of a store ahead of me. I took my chances in running across the street amid the squealing of brakes. The man across the street eyed me curiously. I walked on. Nobody on this side.

A phone. If I could get to a phone I could call Lieutenant Grever. He could send a car, leave the motor running. He would understand. All I would have to do is get in it and go home. I'd thank him later, once I got home, and he could have somebody come and pick up the car. That was the answer. All I needed was a dime.

I searched through my pockets. Not a cent. I had twenty one-dollar bills in my billfold, but I didn't have a cent of change. I knew better than to hope I could get change for a dollar anywhere. I felt like the ghost of Hamlet's father doomed to walk Los Angeles streets, unable to communicate with anyone, unable even to make a phone call.

I could call *collect*. Ridiculous, but true. All I needed to do was find a phone booth. Find one before anything else happened. I hastened my steps. Surely there'd be a phone booth somewhere, one of those outdoor things. I could go in, close the door and call. It was simple and I'd be relatively safe.

I hadn't gone a hundred feet before two men emerged from a shop ahead of me. They were talking agitatedly at each other. O.K., I said to myself. I've learned my lesson. I'll cross the street rather than tangle with you two. But on the other side of the street came two youngsters. Between them was a perfectly harmless looking dog. I looked behind me. A man was walking toward me, cigar in his mouth, reading a paper.

To my left was another passageway. I turned into it, praying I'd meet nobody. But such wasn't to be my luck. At its exit into the alley I nearly bumped into a man, a fat, bareheaded man in a leather apron. He was doing something with a large bucket near a door that opened to the alley.

The fat man took one look at me and swung the bucket. It came up, hit the side of my head and I went reeling. The man came after me, bucket swishing through the air. His eyes were as wild as the dog's, and he was out to kill. I managed to step aside. The bucket—I think it was a paint bucket—hit the side of the building with a horrible crunch and I was glad it wasn't my head again, and he lost his footing.

I jumped, afraid of the bucket, but he'd lost it and was now coming at me, arms flailing. He was a big man, but it wasn't his life that was in danger; it was mine. I struck out with all my strength, hit his shoulder, and we both bounced away. He was back in a moment, and his fist found my cheek and I could sense the cut it caused there, could see the bright flashes it made inside my head. I was down and with a cry he was coming for me. I lifted a foot. He stumbled, crashed into me, his head hitting mine.

My vision blurred. I remember struggling to my feet, weak. I tasted blood. I couldn't see. But I could hear and I stumbled into the alley. I heard a growl behind me. I turned. I saw vaguely the shape of the man who had landed atop me. He was lying where he'd fallen on me, and a brown thing—I could barely make out the white teeth—was coming out of the passageway for me. The dog belonging to the two youngsters.

I don't know how I ever found it, but there was a window a little above street level. I kicked at it, and it moved inward. I remember something about how I felt as I crouched down, how I must have scrambled through that opening to escape the dog behind me. I must have been fast because I didn't lose any more of my trousers. I must have been fast because I fell into where-ever it was.

I hit, thudded to the floor. I didn't know where it was, but it was quiet, it was cool. It was peaceful.

I remember thinking how nice it was before I blacked out completely.

ELEVEN

Somewhere water dripped. Drip ... drip-drip ... drip. If it had had a regular beat it might have lulled me, but its irregularity caught at the edge of my mind and forced me to waken enough to know something was amiss. What I was in wasn't my own bed. And then I thought it more strongly: This isn't my bed! It's no bed at all!

Then I was really, janglingly awake, sitting up, groaning at protesting muscles, trying to see in the darkness. And even as I did this, everything came back in a rush and I looked up to see a gray rectangle that was the window.

Drip ... drip ... drip-drip-drip.

I'd fallen through the window. Not fallen exactly. I'd pushed my way frantically through to escape the dog. My cheek throbbed. I remembered the bucket. I wondered if leather apron still lay sprawled out in the passageway just as I had remained sprawled out in here on—what was it I was on? It wasn't the floor.

I felt under me. Cardboard. I was on several boxes, one leg extending over one of them. I moved cautiously, felt the edge of the box, all the others. I felt farther down. Another box. I crawled down the stack of boxes until I was on concrete. Then I remembered my matches. I brought out a pack of them, struck one.

My surroundings jelled in the brightness. A basement. Cases of beer. I was near a door. I walked over quietly, peered out, holding the flaming match over my head. I saw a sink at the other end of the basement, a dirty sink on either side of which were more boxes. On my left was a wire cage with a door with a big pad-lock. Inside the cage nearly filling it were cases of liquor. Striking match after match, I made my way to the sink. I was thirsty and was going to turn the faucet there, but I suddenly thought the better of it. If anyone was upstairs—and I could see stairs to my right—he would hear the sound of running water. But the beer— even warm beer! Someone had conveniently installed a bottle opener on the wall. The beer was good. So I had another. Nothing to eat all day (nor drink all day) but two bottles of beer.

I felt good again. In fact, I felt clever leaving the way I'd come, and I even thought I ought to try to remember this place, come down and pick up a case of beer sometime. I stood up. It shocked me that it was moonlight and I tried to see what time it was on my wrist watch, but I couldn't see the dial numbers or the hands plainly. It was either ten minutes after ten or ten minutes to two.

I was standing there like a fool, actually pleased with myself when a dark shape hurtled out of the darkness with the most un- holy cry I'd ever heard and impaled itself on my neck. I found myself shouting at the thing on my back, I felt the claws digging in, the searing pain, and I tried to grab its fur and yank in panic. I dislodged it finally. But not until after the cat had scratched my scalp, my hands and my neck. I could see the marks on my hands in the moonlight. I had thrown it from me, thought it would run away, but it had merely stood there for a moment, its back arched, then started for me again.

I ran. I didn't know cats could be so fast. It clawed its way up my trousers and I was forced to hit at it fiercely, heard the cloth rip as it fell. I ran like the wind after that, ran out of the alley, ran past stores bright with lights, past cars, a phantasmagoria of running here and there, past people, into people, hearing gasps, shouts. Then there was another alley, away from them all, down the dark streets, kick the dog, kick the cats, pick up that stick you can use it. Better not come at me, you whoever you are, you'll be sorry. Oh, won't listen, eh? Wham! I told you. Run, run, run as you've never run before and run you did but you tripped on the brick or stone or whatever it was and you ran at an angle and you were going so fast you didn't see the high board fence and your head whammed it hard.

There wasn't any moonlight when I woke this time. My ribs hurt. My head throbbed. Every bone in my body ached. Every- thing came back slowly this time and I was sick, sick without even getting to my feet. I couldn't see well, but I got to my feet, weak, trembling, ready to die. I walked slowly, saw the dog. I felt glad when it turned and trotted off. That was a good dog. The best dog. I came to a lighted street. What street was it I didn't care. I turned down it.

And came to the parking lot.

I saw my car alone near the rear of it.

I was never so glad to see anything in my whole life. I walked—staggered—over to it, pulled open the door, got in. For the first time—in how many hours?—I felt safe safe safe. I loved my car. It was beautiful. It was a fortress. It was the best goddam car in the whole world. And I kept bleeding on the cushions and I hated myself for it. Is that the way to treat a car?

My numb fingers were busy looking for my keys in what pockets I had left. But a funny thing, even though I had pockets left I didn't have anything in them. They were empty.

I remember how it felt to cry, bruised, battered, alone in my lovely car, a prisoner in it, a prisoner in his castle.

But I am safe, I said to myself as I let myself slip sideways into the deliciousness that was sleep, I am safe.

The voice came from a long distance. It was like being talked to from overseas through the first cable laid. The voice said, "Mr. DeMoss, Mr. DeMoss. Wake up." And I shrugged off the hand on my shoulder that was waking me. I wanted to retreat, return to my warm nest of sleep, and I almost did again and again. But the hand was insistent and so was the voice, and when the hand got rougher it jarred sore muscles, and the voice was harsher, more strident, and it rasped on my ears. Would it never go away?

"Mr. DeMoss!"

I had to take a look at whatever it was. Whoever it was, it couldn't be denied, and I moved—and groaned. Everything hurt from my head to my toes, and I kept bumping things in an effort to raise myself. But I finally did manage to get an arm around something and sit up a little, and reluctant eyelids were pulled upward. The light was painfully bright.

It was Gus, the parking lot attendant, standing at the open door of the car. I expected him to shriek in terror or to come at me with a jack handle, and I frankly didn't care which he did, remembering the hideous night, or was it nightmare?

But Gus did neither. He stood there, bright-eyed, clean-cut and neat in his crisp uniform. He wasn't afraid. He wasn't angry.

"Gus," I said thickly, "I love you."

"Mr. DeMoss," he said, "are you all right?"

"Don't talk so loud," I said, bringing a hand up to my head. It was not as large as I thought it would be. It was odd, too, that I could not feel through my hands how it throbbed. In fact, it was odd that I felt anything, considering.

"I'm not talking loud, Mr. DeMoss."

Daylight. What day was this? What time of day? I moved my left forearm, the better to look at my wrist watch. It wasn't there.

Now what had happened to my wrist watch? I stared at the black hairs, saw the faint white line where the watch band had been.

"Mr. DeMoss, you must have had a bad night."

For some reason this set me to laughing. I probably would have become hysterical, except that it hurt too much to laugh. I stopped and looked at the man. He was genuinely concerned.

"Let me repeat, Gus. I love you."

"You ain't over it yet, are you?"

"Yes, I'm over it. What time is it?"

"Just a little after six. I came to open up and here you are. You sleep here all night, Mr. DeMoss?"

"I guess so." Why try to explain?

"Can you drive all right?"

"Sure." It would take a large portion of will power, but I'd drive. Except that when I looked for my keys they weren't there. No wrist watch, no keys, no billfold, no nothing. Except the clothes I wore. And they were a mess. "I could drive," I said, "except I don't have my keys."

"You did have a night." Gus shook his head. "I don't think I ever saw anybody look so bad. Sure you ain't got your key?"

"Yes." My tongue worked against a loose tooth. I wondered vaguely how that happened.

"I could wire around it," Gus said, "but I hate to do a thing like that. Ain't you got one at home or something? It's going to start getting busy in here pretty soon."

"Gus, get me a cup of coffee, huh?"

"Sure thing, Mr. DeMoss. You wait right there. Ah, I'd get back in and close the door if I was you."

I got the idea and did as he said. He was back in a matter of minutes with a two-cup carton of coffee. It was scalding hot and I had difficulty holding it, but it was good. I could feel strength returning along all the muscles and nerves. Once I caught a glimpse of myself in the rearview mirror. I wasn't very pretty. I had a bad bruise and cut on my cheek, scratches over almost every inch of my face, a beautiful black eye. My hands looked like a plumber's helper's. A few minutes ago they had trembled. Now they were quiet.

"You got blood all over the seat. You get in a fight or something?"

I managed to smile. It was like smiling with a new face, one that hadn't been cracked yet, like a new book. I could feel the stretch and strain of it and it didn't last long. "Cats and dogs, mostly," I said, shuddering a little.

Gus said, "Why don't you take a cab home? I'd run you, but I can't leave here."

I told him I didn't have a cent and he gave me ten dollars.

"I know you're good for it," he said. He grinned. "Besides, I got your car."

I don't think the cabdriver would have taken me home if I hadn't shown him the ten dollar bill first. And all the way there he kept looking at me in his mirror. But I'll say this for that hackie: He didn't say a thing.

I walked up to my apartment house as big as life. I didn't care what I looked like, I was so glad to get home. I knew there was going to be difficulty because I didn't have a key, but even that didn't seem an insurmountable problem. I merely looked up Hoskins, the super, and I let him stare at me popeyed before I said, "I've lost my key somewhere."

"They've been looking for you, Mr. DeMoss," he said.

"They?" Lieutenant Grever, probably.

"I let the lady in last night. Didn't you ever get home?"

"The lady?"

"Sure. I'll let you in. Maybe she's still there."

She was. Anne was curled up asleep on the davenport, the prettiest picture I'd ever seen. Hoskins wanted to come in, but I nudged him out and closed the door after him. I didn't care what he thought. I was past caring what anybody thought.

The clicking of the door shut woke her. Her eyes opened with a start, staring for a long moment. Then she sat up as if jolted by electricity, eyes wide.

"Phil!" Her eyes jumped over my figure, settled on my eyes. Then she was in my arms. "Oh, Phil! Whatever happened to you?"

The pain of her embrace was almost more than I could bear, but my love was even greater.

"Easy, honey," I said, gently detaching her. Something was wrong with my ribs all right.

"You're hurt," she said.

"My head is bloody, and not entirely unbowed," I quipped.

"Your suit is ruined."

"The only undamaged thing about me is my psyche."

She slid my suitcoat over my shoulders. "You're going to take off those clothes," she said. "You're going to take a bath."

"I will, but I've got to get my strength up first. I haven't had anything to eat since night before last."

"Oh, Phil!" That galvanized her into action. She forgot how I looked, took me to the kitchen, insisted I tell her everything that had happened while she prepared our breakfast. Sitting there with Anne moving about my kitchen was wonderful, and while I tried not to dwell on the terror aspects of it, I told her everything.

She punctuated it with "Oh, darling!" and "How awful!" and several times she felt moved to come over and cradle my head against her breasts. I didn't mind that at all. Anne was a wonderful girl. If I had ever had any doubt about her love, which I never had, it would have been erased right then and there.

Then, while I ate, she told me Lieutenant Grever had tried to get in touch with me and had called her after calling my office, Selma telling him I hadn't been in.

"He's been terribly worried and so have I. I came over here in the afternoon and waited and waited, and Lieutenant Grever called again and again."

She said the police had started a search for me, that Glenn Klock, Clifford Ellis and Jake Hardy had organized their own hunt. And suddenly she stopped. "You had it, but you don't have it any more." Her eyes were bright. "That's something."

"It's everything," I said. "I wouldn't be here if I still had it."

"I know it must be pretty horrible. What do you think it is?"

I told her I hadn't the slightest idea, and we tossed guesses around. But we didn't come up with anything.

She called Lieutenant Grever while I took a bath. Lieutenant Grever said he'd get in touch with the others in the Forty-two Club, saying they'd been bothering him about every hour on the hour for news. He said he was coming over and he'd bring a doctor with him. She told me all that through the bathroom door.

I was a mess, but I don't think I had any broken bones. I came out of the bathroom with bandages and merthiolate and gauze and tape. Anne did an efficient job on my cuts.

She saw the dark blue marks on my lips, chin, forehead, eye and ribs, and said, "Somebody must have kicked you."

"Kicked me when I was down, I guess. Got a loose tooth, too." I wiggled it for her. "No wrist watch or anything left. First time I was ever rolled."

"You poor darling." She reached for me. I was hoping that would happen. The breakfast had given me strength. I was able to squeeze back this time.

"You've got a beard," she said. "Or at least the start of one."

"I'll shave."

"You don't have to for me. Besides, won't it be hard around all those scratches and cuts?"

"I'll look less like a sourdough if I do. I don't feel myself this way. Anyway, Grever's coming."

"And a doctor."

"I don't need a doctor."

"You can't tell, Phil. You've been hurt pretty badly."

I kissed her again for good measure, told her I'd be a minute and went into the bathroom. It wasn't easy shaving; it probably would have been easier with an electric shaver, but I managed, and my appearance was certainly vastly improved. The after-shave lotion really got down in the scratches and cuts and I stood there grimacing until the pain of it abated. I was covered with sweat by that time and felt as if I needed another bath.

I was wholly unprepared for what happened when I went back into the living room to show Anne the improvement.

She rose from her chair, took one look at me, put her hand to her neck, her mouth working agitatedly. She was terrified.

"No, Phil! Phil!" she cried as I took a step toward her. Her eyes showed her agony. She swallowed hard, retreated toward the front door. "Please! Oh, God, Phil!" And uttering a little cry, she turned, opened the door and rushed through it, the door swinging shut behind her.

TWELVE

I had it again. For a few hours I had been free of it; Gus had talked to me and hadn't noticed anything other than my appear-ance, and Anne had been there and we'd talked and she had pre-pared breakfast. But now it was back. In full force, too, if Anne's face was any indication.

I felt fear enveloping me like a shroud. It turned to panic as I lived again all the agonizing moments of the night before, the senseless running, attacks by the leather-aproned man, the dogs and cats, the bone weariness of waking in the middle of the night in a dark place and the final resignation and wandering. My heart pounded and I could feel the ooze of cold sweat from every pore; I knew exactly how others felt about me now, and for a few moments I was filled with self-reproach, self-effacement. I just wasn't equal to it. I couldn't go through that all over again. I absolutely could not.

Now I felt as Poley had. As Ernst had.

But it was over in a few moments—my panic. Common sense said nothing could happen as long as I stayed in the house, and the feeling of dread ebbed away. I was Philip DeMoss again. And I had just seen Anne Whiting walk out of the door. Well, at least we knew what it was. I hoped what Anne had witnessed would create no trauma. I didn't want a wife who would remem-ber a thing like that every time she looked at me. I was sure she wouldn't, and I convinced myself of it as I recalled how helpful she had been, how concerned and solicitous. It touched me that she had stayed the afternoon and night in the apartment waiting for me, worried about me. How many girls would have done that?

I walked to the window. Downstairs I saw Anne on the sidewalk talking to two men. One was Lieutenant Grever. A police car was behind him. Another man stood beside Grever. Probably the doctor. Of course it was the doctor. He had his little black bag. Anne was talking, gesturing. Grever was nodding, and he looked up at the window. I didn't know if he could really see me there, but I waved anyway. He waved back. Then, to my surprise, he and the doctor got in the police car and drove away. That I didn't understand. Anne stood looking after them for a few moments, then started back for the apartment. I hoped she wouldn't try to come up. But she did. She stopped at the door.

"Phil?"

"Yes. Where did Grever go?"

"I told him you'd been all right but that you suddenly got it again. Should I come in?"

"No. You'd better stay out there. The door will stop it from coming through to you. What about Grever?"

"He's going down the street to telephone."

"Oh." Silence. I wondered what she was doing. In a moment she said, "Are you all right, Phil?"

"I feel fine. It's the damndest thing." I did feel good, except for the various aches and pains. I wanted my pipe. They'd taken that, too. Well, I had others. "I'm going to get a pipe," I told her. "I can think better with it."

"You be careful," Anne said. "Is the back door locked?"

"I left it locked. It must still be."

"Don't let anybody in. Lieutenant Grever doesn't want anybody inside."

"O.K." I went to my bedroom, picked up one of my old pipes, filled it with tobacco from a cannister, lighted it. I ought to call Selma, I thought. I looked at my wrist. No wrist watch, of course. I looked at the dresser clock. Nearly eight thirty. She'd be in the office soon. I chuckled to think how cold her voice would be. Only she'd have worried, too, wouldn't she?

The phone rang. It was Grever.

"How do you feel?" he asked.

"Like the Wreck of the Hesperus."

"The wreck of the what?"

"Never mind. Oh, I feel all right considering that several people and assorted cats and dogs tried to make mincemeat out of me."

"Anne told me a little bit of it. Seemed better to call than to try to come up or talk through a door. Do you think you need any protection?"

"My greatest enemy is myself, Lieutenant."

"You're going to be a good boy and stay put now?"

"After last night, I'm staying put, believe me."

"Good."

Then he wanted to know what happened and I told him. I spared no detail, but even as I said it it sounded like too much. Could all that have really happened? I wondered if he believed me.

Later, when I'd finished, he said, "Now let me get this straight. You were all right this morning up until a little while ago. Right?"

"Right."

"Then the effect does wear off during the night?"

"Yes. Herb had it figured that way."

"I think so. Miss Whiting didn't notice anything strange?"

"Just my cuts and bruises."

"She said you were a sight." Pause. "You took a bath?"

"That's right."

"You were all right after that?"

"Sure I was all right."

"Then you went back into the bathroom?" The lieutenant's voice seemed a little agitated. I wondered why.

I got a glimmer of it myself when I said slowly, "Yes, then I went into the bathroom again."

Lieutenant Grever was exultant. "And you shaved?"

"Yes. I see what you mean." Now I was jarred a bit. "Either the shaving cream——"

"You use a safety razor?"

"—or the after-shave lotion. I used the same bar of soap for my bath."

"That's it, DeMoss. The shaving lotion."

"The shaving lotion? Why couldn't it be the shaving cream?"

"Because," Grever said calmly, "part of the shards of glass picked up at the scene of Dr. Lincoln's murder belonged to a bottle of shaving lotion."

"I see." Yes, I could see it all now as it fell into place so ridiculously simple. Poley McGowan, Ernst Mollinauer and Herb Lincoln—they all shaved and all used after-shave lotion. That's why they got it. That's why the kids didn't get it, why their wives didn't get it. Each morning they'd shave—they had nothing else to do after they got it the first time—and they'd only start the whole thing over again.

I remembered that talk with Ellen McGowan then. Poley had taken to drinking, had let his whiskers grow. He had a remission then, a time when he did emit whatever it was he emitted when he applied the after-shave lotion. Herb was right. Somehow whatever it was in the bottle, when it was spread on the face, was absorbed, interacted with the sweat glands or something under the skin, and produced a vapor or something that became an aura of fear.

I'd read about how animals can smell fear. I'd heard experienced soldiers tell about the odor of fear. So the body is capable of doing strange things. Only in this case whatever was produced by the body produced a violent reaction in others.

"You still there?"

I must have been quiet a long time. "Yes. I was thinking."

"You've got the picture?"

"I've got it. I see how it was done now."

"You've got the shaving lotion," he said, "so I'll tell you what I want you to do. I want you to wrap it in newspapers, plenty of newspapers, and throw it from the window when I get back there. I'll try to catch it, but I don't want it to break if I miss it. I used to be a good ballplayer, but that was a good many years ago and I don't want to take the chance."

"You want to get it analyzed, is that it?"

"Yes. Dr. Lincoln was going to do it. Now it seems it's up to me to get it done."

I had thought of something else. "Lieutenant," I said, "there are three other bottles of shaving lotion. Maybe you ought to pick them up, too."

Grever whistled. "I'd forgotten about them." Pause. "No, on second thought I think I'll leave them where they are. It's taking a chance I know, but I don't want to tip my hand just yet."

"I hope nobody takes a notion to use any of it."

"So do I."

"Another thing."

"Yes?"

"Who put the overalls in Mrs. Murphy's chowder?"

Grever laughed. "A good question. Maybe it's you."

"If you'd seen me last night you wouldn't say a thing like that. In fact, if you could see me now you wouldn't think so."

"Strange thing, DeMoss," he said heartily, "I happen to believe you."

After the call I lighted my pipe again and walked to the front door. "You still there, Anne?"

"Sure, I am. Your ever faithful. If there were two of me, the other would be at the back door."

"What are you doing, just standing there?"

"No, silly. I'm sitting on the floor with my shoes off."

93

"I'll bet you look nice."

"I'm glad you think so."

"Have I told you lately I love you?"

"Not for a day or so. Do you?"

"Madly."

"Funny, I feel the same way about you. Was that the lieutenant who called?"

"Yes. He's coming back soon."

"He is? Don't you think I can do a good job of guarding your door?"

I told her why he was coming back.

Anne said, "After the horse is stolen."

"It's not too late. There are Ellis, Hardy and Klock to consider. And maybe some other people. Who knows?"

"No, just two."

"Two?"

"Clifford Ellis, Jake Hardy or Glenn Klock—one of them did it. That leaves the other two."

"I still can't believe any of them could have done it."

"My intuition is pretty strong this morning."

"Who does it say it is?"

"Jake Hardy."

"Hardy? For heaven's sake, Anne, it couldn't be."

"Why not?"

I didn't know. I said, "It just couldn't be, that's all. Suppose you tell me why you think it could."

"I just told you. Intuition. One doesn't question intuition, darling, remember?"

A small pebble or stone hit the front window with a *tic*. I went over, raised the window. Grever was standing on the grass. He said, "You got it ready?"

"I've been talking to Anne. Wait a minute." I went to the bathroom, opened the medicine cabinet, gingerly took out my bottle of shaving lotion. It looked innocent enough. Just green liquid sloshing around inside. I went to the kitchen, wrapped it heavily in newspapers and put it in a paper bag. Then I returned to the window, dropped it to Grever. He caught it expertly.

"Not bad, eh?" He grinned.

"No minor league catch," I said. "Let's hear what it is if you find out."

"Let you know," he said, strolling across the lawn.

I went back to Anne. It was so pleasant talking to her that I forgot all about Selma until she called. She wasn't angry at all, but of course she shouldn't have been. In fact, she was warmer on this day than I had ever known her to be.

"I'm so glad you're all right," she said. "I—I was really worried yesterday. I managed to get out the Ryan papers, and—but I can tell you that when you get here. What I mean is, even though I was working I couldn't help but wondering—well, Lieutenant Grever. . . ." I heard a sniffle from the other end of the line and it startled me to think that Selma really did care, personally. I chided myself for all the times I'd thought she was cold and so professionally efficient and that was all. I would have liked to say something warm to her but I couldn't find the words, thinking of Anne sitting on the floor in front of my door.

"I'm not coming in today either," I said. "I—I'm not myself. I had a rough time."

She wanted to know what I meant by that and what happened, but I said I'd be in on Monday to fill her in and tell her all about it. I told her she had my complete trust and that I felt the office couldn't be in more competent hands. She seemed happy enough to break off with that. I made a mental note to see what I could do about a raise for that girl. She deserved it.

When I went back to talking with Anne, she said, "You shaved the day before yesterday—Wednesday—didn't you?"

"Of course. I'm a big boy now, remember?"

"I mean here. You used the same bottle of shaving lotion?"

"Yes." I couldn't remember it exactly, but I must have used it. "I was all right then. But then yesterday morning I used it and the reaction set in."

"Yes," Anne said. "So whatever it is was put in the bottle between Wednesday morning and Thursday morning."

"That seems logical. But nobody broke in here, as they did in Herb Lincoln's apartment."

"Didn't they?"

"The only place anyone could really come in is through the back door or a back window."

"You don't follow me, do you?"

"I'd follow you anywhere, darling. Lead on."

"Oh, stop being a ninny. Whoever put the stuff in the lotion bottle walked through your front door Wednesday night."

Of course. Lieutenant Grever, the Klocks, Ellis and Hardy— plus Anne and myself—had all walked through the door. One of them had gone to the bathroom, put the stuff in the bottle. But then everyone had visited the room.

"Phil?"

"I was thinking. Somebody did it that night. But who?"

Just then the phone rang. Lieutenant Grever again.

"Something just occurred to me," he said. "Let's not advertise about the lotion. We've got information the criminal doesn't know we have. We can use it to good advantage at the proper time and in the proper place."

"I told Anne about it."

"I wish you hadn't."

"She won't tell anyone about it."

"Tell her that, will you? One more thing."

"Yes, Lieutenant?"

"In case you're interested, I asked for a volunteer down here and one of our rookies went into a conference room and dabbed a little of that lotion on his face."

"Poor guy."

"It's every bit as bad as has been said. His name is Tinwood, Archie Tinwood. He's got a lot of magazines and newspapers in there to read, says he wants to go through it again tomorrow. Says we're all nuts. But I've got things to do. Just remember to keep it quiet."

I told Anne. She said she'd be quiet.

"Nobody to tell it to out here anyway," she said. "Never realized before how dismal a corridor can be. Just this carpet, walls and doors and a ceiling. No, there's a window down the hall."

"Still sitting?"

"Yes, and I'm getting tired. If I had a pillow, I'd stretch out."

"I'd rather have you inside. I could go to the kitchen or the bedroom. Maybe it wouldn't be so bad. You could take the calls."

"It *is* dull out here."

The phone rang before we could arrange it. I answered.

"Hello?"

Silence. I could hear the intake of breath.

"Hello," I said again, a little gruffly. I don't like to play games on the phone.

"Phil?"

"Yes. Who's this?"

"Jake. Jake Hardy."

He didn't sound like himself. Something was wrong. He seemed to strangle his voice. I tried to be casual by saying, "Thanks for organizing a hunting party for me."

All he said was, "Phil?"

"Something's wrong. What is it, Jake?"

More breathing into the mouthpiece. "Tried to call Cliff. He wasn't home." At least that's what it sounded as if he said. His words were a little slurred and strung together. "Then I thought of you. The lieutenant said to get in touch."

"Get in touch?"

"I've got the thing. I've got that plague thing, Phil."

"You've got it?" I repeated foolishly. "When did you get it?"

"I don't know."

"How do you know you've got it?"

"When I got out of the car at the office. Then I knew I had it." He was sounding more in control of himself. "Guys I knew for years—you should have seen their faces, Phil."

"I know." He was telling me.

"I started back for my car, but I got in a fight with Andy—he's my assistant out here. I think he'd have killed me if I hadn't knocked him out. I was still winded when I got home in the car. The lieutenant said to go home."

"That's right. You stay there, Jake."

"I feel awful about Andy."

"He couldn't help it."

"What do I do now, Phil? I can't stay here. I got to get down there at the plant. I don't know how bad off Andy is."

"Can't you call? Can't you take care of things by phone?"

Pause. "I guess so. I'm all done in. Thing like this never happened to me before. It's awful."

"I know. I went through it yesterday."

"You went through it, Phil? You mean you had it?"

"But good. I didn't know I had it until I got too far away from my car to get back to it."

"So that's what happened to you! Are you all right now?"

"No, I've got it again, Jake, but I'll be all right as long as I stay in the apartment." I was on the point of telling him about the shaving lotion, but I remembered Grever's admonition. Hardy might call Clifford Ellis or Glenn Klock and tell them.

And now one of them was guilty.

"I got a bottle here," Jake was saying. "I think I'll drink the whole damn thing."

"It won't help." I was glad I hadn't told him about the lotion. If he got drunk he might blab it all around. "We're just lucky we know what it is—I mean as long as we stay cooped up. You know what I mean." I nearly spilled it then again. "You stay in, Jake. I'll call Grever and tell him."

"I wish you would. I'm not setting a foot out of here. You do the same. I figure we'll end up like the others if we do."

"You're right, Jake. I'll keep in touch and you do the same, hear?"

"O.K., Phil. But I don't like it."

After the call I went to the door, said to Anne, "Scratch one suspect."

"Who?"

"Jake Hardy. He's got it."

"Somebody got to him, too, then. That leaves Glenn and Cliff."

"Right. I'll unlock the door and go to the kitchen. If you can stand it, I'll talk to you from there. I think I've got an idea."

THIRTEEN

My idea was simple, and I explained it to Anne in the living room as I sat in the kitchen. Once I heard her reopen the window through which I had thrown the package of lotion to Grever. When I asked her what she was doing, she said it had become a little stuffy and she wanted a little air. But I knew what had happened. Confined to the apartment as we were, some of the fear-and-hate-engendering vapor must have been wafted to her. I had no idea how strong it was, but I admired her for not mentioning it.

"Anne," I said, "we know either Glenn or Cliff is guilty of this whole thing."

"You've given up on Lula, then?"

"Lula? You know I never really considered her."

"Well, I don't know what to think since my intuition turned out to be so unreliable. I was sure it was Jake Hardy. I can't work up much enthusiasm about Cliff or Glenn."

I poured myself a little coffee from the pot on the stove, asked her if she wanted some, but she said she didn't. "I want to hear your idea," she said.

I stirred the coffee and thought out loud. "Just this: Suppose I get the bottle of lotion from Grever. I take it over to Glenn's. I tell him I've got a new lotion I'd like him to try. I show him the bottle. If he winces, turns away, doesn't want to try it, he's the guilty man."

"I see. Next you try Cliff, if Glenn shows no suspicion. Right?"

"Right." It seemed very logical to me. "Next I drive up to San Benuto. I know by this time Cliff is guilty, so all I need in order to make sure is to see him refuse to try it."

Anne was silent so long I asked, "You still there?"

"Yes, I'm still here."

"What do you think of the idea?"

"Not much."

I was rankled. "What's wrong with it?"

"First off, Phil, wouldn't it be rather silly to be coming over to somebody's house just to have him try a little shaving lotion?"

"I'd try to work it in logically."

"You'd try, but it just doesn't seem right to me. Besides, suppose Glenn decides to try it, for example? You've got him dosed with the stuff, he has to stay home and Lula goes out of her mind. Neither of them would ever speak to you again."

"I'd have to take that chance."

"And then, suppose you go up to Cliff's place. You try the same thing. He takes some of it, spreads it on his face. Then he's got it. Then where are you?"

"Well . . ." It did seem a lot to ask two friends to do. Especially if it should turn out that neither of them had anything to do with it. But what else was there?

"Let's build on it," Anne said.

"O.K.," I said. "Start building."

"You don't even know that Lieutenant Grever would let you have the lotion again."

"I could ask him for it."

"He's having it analyzed, isn't he?"

"That's what he said."

"So probably he doesn't have it."

"O.K.," I said again. "So he doesn't have it." It *had* sounded like a good idea.

"Oh, don't give up, Phil. Basically your idea is sound."

"Thank you for small favors."

"No, I mean it. It really is."

"That still doesn't save it."

"Phil, the trouble is, you haven't gone far enough. You don't need the shaving lotion at all."

"I don't?"

"No. All you need is an identical bottle. You can pick one up at a drugstore. You confront Glenn with it. If he isn't hesitant about putting some on his hands or face and smelling it, then you know he's not the one. The same with Clifford Ellis."

"Yes," I said grudgingly. The coffee was bitter. "Yes, I could see how that would work." Now why hadn't I thought of it?

"Another thing," she went on, "your timing is wrong."

I didn't say anything. It was turning into Anne's idea. I let her go on building it.

"I'd be suspicious if somebody came to me and asked me to try something. Especially with the situation as it stands now. Don't you think they'd think you were a little odd, suddenly dropping in?"

"I suppose you're right," I conceded.

"It has to be casual. It has to be worked out logically. You won't get a decent reaction unless you do. Still another thing:

You'd have to take your chance that Glenn was home if you dropped by. The same with Clifford Ellis. I have a better idea."

"'Proceed,'" I said.

"My folks have a lodge at Lake Arrowhead. Today is Friday. Why not invite Ellis and the Klocks to the lodge for the weekend? On Sunday morning you can go into the bit about the shaving lotion. By breakfast time you ought to have the answer."

"I don't know." I was sceptical. "What reason would I have to ask them there? And what reason would they have for going?"

"You've been through a lot and so have they. What could seem more natural than getting away for the weekend? To escape it all. I feel sure the Klocks would want to go. I don't know about Ellis. But we might convince him he ought to."

I nodded, just as if Anne were in the kitchen with me. "That sounds reasonable. But what about Jake Hardy? He ought to go too. I hate to think of him renewing the aura each morning after he shaves, sitting cooped up in his house just because I didn't tell him about the shaving lotion."

"The lieutenant said not to tell anyone."

"That was before I knew about Jake. I don't think the lieutenant would care if I told Jake, and besides, I think we ought to invite Jake, too. That way we'd have some help. We might need it, you know. Guilty people can be pretty nasty when they're cornered."

"That makes sense. But I think we ought to iron it all out before we start calling people."

"Right." I found myself nodding again.

We talked of ways and means and strategy for a while. This thing would have to appear as a friendly gathering in a mountain lodge, a real escape from our problems. Congenial people, friends, a fireplace, a few drinks, visiting. And as for my appearance, we invented a story about how I'd spent yesterday out of town, how I'd flown up to San Francisco, and on my return became involved in a street fight as I was passing by.

"It's not good," Anne said, "but because it's not good it might even be convincing."

"One of them will know at the lodge," I said. "The guilty one will know I didn't get into a fight just passing by."

"Let's hope by Sunday breakfast it won't make any difference."

The ringing of the phone nearly jolted me out of my chair. We had become so accustomed to speaking in low tones, straining to hear each other, the sharp jangling of the bell seemed louder than normal.

As we had agreed in advance, Anne left the living room via the front door, while I answered the phone. It was Glenn.

"Hi," he said. "Are you all right?"

"Sure, I'm all right. What did you expect?"

"We were looking for you last night. What happened?"

I gave out with the song and dance about leaving late Wednesday for San Francisco and returning late Thursday only to get involved in a fight. "Damndest thing that ever happened to me. Before it was over everybody was jumping me."

"That's terrible," Glenn said. "Were they kids? Sometimes the leather jacket crowd can get awful tough."

I coughed to give myself time to think "It—it was dark and it all happened so fast, I don't know how old they were. My guess is they were youngsters, though."

"Where did it happen?"

"Where did it happen?" I was stalling for time. Where *did* it happen? I had no idea it would get so involved.

"Yes. Did it happen here in L.A.?"

"Uh-huh."

"Whereabouts in L.A.?"

"Well . . . You know where my office is. Well, there's a parking lot near there where I keep my car. It—it was in an alley near. Heard you fellows organized a search party."

"Oh, we didn't do much. Looked in all the obvious places. We left Anne at your place. She was supposed to call when you turned up. But Grever called this morning. Did you see her?"

"Yes. I'm sorry about it. I should have let someone know."

"Seems funny you didn't let your secretary know, Phil. Did you know she was as worried as the rest of us?"

"Yes. Poor Selma. It was an unforgivable oversight."

"Business trip, eh?"

"Yes, Glenn."

"I would have called sooner, but there were some rush proofs. Lieutenant Grever called me at home before breakfast. Did you know he was out looking too?"

"Yes." I laughed. I was amazed; it didn't even sound forced. "He gave me the devil for it, don't think he didn't."

"We're all jumpy. I seem to be dividing my time between thinking about those of us left and my work here at the office. Yesterday you had us all scared. We thought perhaps you were the newest victim. Lula was convinced you were."

"She was?"

"Yes. It really gets her, this whole business."

"Say, Glenn," I said little more vigorously, "thinking of Lula reminds me." I went into the business about the weekend at the lodge at Lake Arrowhead. He was a little dubious.

"I'm not sure Lula even wants us to leave the house, Phil."

"Just pleasure," I said. "Just to get away from it all."

"Well, I'll have to call her first."

That was the best I could do. But in a few minutes he called back and said she thought it was a great idea. There was a little fumbling while I got the route to the lodge from Anne outside the door, but I got it and gave it to him. He said they'd drive up in the afternoon, getting to the lodge around two. I said that was fine. Now I had to get Cliff there.

I put in a person-to-person call to him in San Benuto. He didn't sound glad to hear from me at all.

"I thought they'd drag you up from some old creek bottom or something," he said. "And I was thinking good riddance. Give the young barristers a break. What made you change your mind?"

"Change my mind?"

"Sure. How come you didn't commit suicide?"

"Why should I?"

"Oh, come on. Nobody gets this plague or whatever it is and disappears from the heart of the city the way you did without something hideous happening to him."

"What makes you think I had the plague?"

"Didn't you?"

"No."

"Well." Cliff sounded surprised. "All that weeping for nothing. I fancied a meeting of the Forty-two Club, only we were going to call it the Unscathed Triumvirate, there being only three of us left. Even that became almost too much to bear, just Jake Hardy, Glenn Klock and I. Goes to prove the good die young." He laughed. "I guess maybe I am glad to hear your voice. You'll put a little pep back in the club. What did happen to you?"

I told him about San Francisco, about the scuffle in the street. He stopped me halfway through it.

"O.K., junior, you can come off that jazz right now. Don't bug me, friend. I'm not that naive. You don't have to tell me a damn thing if you don't want to. Was there a woman involved? Never mind. Let's just skip it, shall we?"

"You don't believe it?"

"That story wouldn't beguile an idiot child. Next time, please let everybody know you're just dropping out of sight for a day or two. You had everybody standing on his head."

"All right, Cliff. As a special favor to you, I'll let you know in advance. But seriously, there's something I want to ask you." And I told him about the lodge at Lake Arrowhead.

"Now why are you inviting me there?" he asked. "Nobody invites me anywhere. I'm a party killer, didn't you know that?"

102

"This isn't a party. Just be yourself. Everybody knows you. Nobody cares how you act."

He sighed. "That was the trouble with the Forty-two Club. Everybody in it knew me too well. Who's going to be there?"

"The Klocks, Jake and Anne and I."

"Might as well," he said. I told him how to get there and at what time. He said, "Anything new on the plague?"

"Nothing I know of."

"Maybe it's all over. I hope so."

Next I put in a call to Jake Hardy. The phone rang and rang. I couldn't believe he wouldn't be there, but after I'd put the call through a second time and still got no response, there was nothing to do but accept it.

"Jake's left the house," I told Anne through the door. "I just called his place. No answer."

"He shouldn't have done that."

"You're telling me. He doesn't know what can happen to him. I can just picture him running through alleys, from people, cats and dogs. God only knows where he is right now."

"You'd better call Lieutenant Grever. You promised Jake you would."

I did. Grever seemed annoyed that I hadn't called him earlier about Jake Hardy.

"I could have got somebody from the sheriff's office to look in on him. Now maybe it's going to be too late. I tried to get him earlier to tell him about you, but that's when he must have been out."

I told him I was going to tell Jake about the shaving lotion. Grever said that wouldn't have been wrong, that it might even have saved his life, if he failed to survive being out of the house. He said he'd call if he got any word from the sheriff's office. I told him Cliff might be able to help, but Grever said it would be better to let the sheriff's office handle it exclusively.

"Amateurs always mess up things like this," he said.

I didn't say anything. Maybe I should have. Maybe he was right. But the trap had been baited and I didn't want to call that off. I wanted to see which of two men was going to walk into it.

FOURTEEN

Somehow the hours of that Friday crept by. I am not much of a stay-at-home—at least I hadn't been—and that, plus the fact that I had to stay in the kitchen with Anne in the living room gave the whole an air of unreality. But Anne and I became better acquainted, and when we could stop thinking about the bizarre nature of the arrangement long enough, we actually enjoyed it.

We had lunch sent in, Anne accepting it at the front door, then leaving for a stroll while I went in for my share of it. Then she returned, I ate in the kitchen and she ate in the living room. We did the same thing for dinner, and before the day was over we felt at home moving around like chess pieces. I was bushed early and Anne could see I was, so she left. I agreed to pick her up in the morning, insistent as Anne was to leave plenty of time to prepare the lodge for guests. I was to pick her up right after breakfast.

The last thing I did before I turned in was to call Lieutenant Grever. They said he was off duty. I hung up. Somehow I had gotten the idea that Grever worked twenty-four hours a day. Well, it could wait. I only hoped the sheriff's deputies would locate Jake Hardy before something happened to him.

I fell asleep the moment my head hit my pillow and didn't wake up until eight the next morning. I took a shower, shaved, prepared breakfast, and got out to the car before I thought of Hardy again. By then it was too late to call, so I started for Pasadena. Halfway there I got the chilling thought that perhaps something more than shaving lotion was involved—I had shaved that morning, had come in contact with no one so far. I settled it by stopping the car and buying a newspaper. The clerk in the store took my money without giving me a second look. I relaxed again.

Anne was waiting for me on the front porch of the Whiting house with its curving crushed-rock drive. My old Chevvy seemed a little out of place on it, as it always did, but I was rewarded by a big smile from Anne and the warmest kiss I'd ever got. I forgot the car.

"Back to normal," Anne said when we caught our breaths. "Thank heaven for that."

"I don't know about that," I said, drawing her to me again. "I think I'm running a temperature."

She laughed and broke away. "Let's not push it any higher, Phil."

Well, plenty of time for things like that later. Next we were out on the road. I stopped at the first highway telephone booth and called Grever. I was informed he was not in the office. I decided to call him later.

It was a wonderful day. The sky was a deep blue, marred only by a jet trail here and there. We could see for miles, which in itself was unusual. Trees were green, mountains purple, and the road bright and clean. Death seemed very far away, and it did not seem possible that we were keeping a rendezvous with someone who had initiated action which had led to the deaths of three friends. And when I thought about Hardy I wondered if, by this time, it was four deaths. Perhaps Grever was out of the office because he'd been called to the sheriff's office because they'd found Jake. Well, no matter. I'd have a little surprise for Grever Sunday morning. I'd be able to hand him the guilty man and the proof. Then it would all be over and those of us left would be able to take up our lives where they had been interrupted.

"You seem worried," Anne said.

"Not worried. Just thinking."

"I don't want to dash any cold water on this thing," she went on, "but I just wonder if we shouldn't have let Lieutenant Grever in on it."

"Can't change that now."

She was silent for a long time before she said, "You know what I hope, Phil?"

"What?"

"I hope neither of them did it."

"Well, I hope so too, but I'm afraid that would put us back where we started." A moment later I said, "Somebody put something in those lotion bottles. And it wasn't a creature from outer space."

"I wish it were. For all his sharpness, I like Cliff after all. And Glenn Klock—well, he seems such a nice, harmless guy, so worried about everything. He and Lula. It would break her heart if he turned out to be the one."

I shook my head. "I just don't understand how either of them could have developed it. I don't think Cliff knows the first thing about chemistry, and Glenn doesn't have a hateful bone in his body. All his time goes into those encyclopedias."

"There's always Lula," Anne said. "I don't want to betray my sex, and murder seems more of a man's game, but she's always interested in taking up something new. Maybe she's taken up an extracurricular activity nobody knows about, such as toxics."

"Intuition again?"

"Not really. Just thinking."

The Whiting lodge was hidden deep in a dense growth of trees. It was a two-story structure, the bedrooms being upstairs, and wide windowpanes in the rear of the house affording a fine view of a mountain stream. It had been built with a rustic motif, but it was modern inside, including an electric kitchen. I couldn't understand why the Whitings didn't live there all year around.

"My parents did live here one year," Anne said, "but they missed city life. Gets pretty lonely. Now it's only a week end now and then. They were going to come up this weekend, but I talked them out of it."

"What do they think of what we're doing?"

"I got a couple sidelong looks, but that's all."

"They must trust me."

Anne smiled. "They trust me, Phil."

"Oh."

We spent the rest of the morning tidying up, sweeping branches and twigs off the patio and porches. A little before noon we went into town for food and to buy the all-important bottle of shaving lotion. By half past one we were ready.

The Klocks were first to arrive, and they fell in love with the place at once. Glenn took me to one side to tell me I was lucky to be marrying Anne Whiting.

"A place like this, Phil," he said. "You've got it made."

I told him I was marrying Anne, not the lodge. I also told him I only knew about the place from things that had been mentioned, that I'd never been here before.

"If I were you I'd be here every weekend," he said. "I could get a lot of work done. No traffic, no interruptions. Maybe even no TV to interfere." He looked around.

I hadn't thought of it, but there was no television. I said, "I'll speak to Mr. Whiting. Maybe he'll sell you the place."

Glenn grinned. "Wait about ten more years. Maybe the Klocks will have some money then."

It was all perfectly normal and natural. Because it was so, it was somehow disquieting.

A little later Cliff drove up in his Corvette. "Say," he said, looking the place over, "I've always wanted a place like this. I could really write here."

"A blonde hanging over your shoulder?" I said.

"I suppose," he said, "that you're one of those fellows who thinks that doesn't help. Where do you suppose I get my inspirations?"

And so it went. A friendly little gathering. Everybody drinking a little, not too much, and late in the afternoon preparations for charcoal-broiled steaks. When it was over we sat around in the living room watching the flames in the fireplace. All very cozy, very disarming. Relaxing. Even Cliff was less vitriolic than usual. It seemed a terrible thing that the pleasant time would, in a matter of hours, be marred by pinning guilt on one of them. I hated myself for the necessity of it, but at the same time I would never forget my night in the alley, and remembering that made what I planned to do seem less regrettable.

I am sure the Klocks and Clifford Ellis went to bed with clear minds. I bade Anne good night, only to turn and toss most of the night. I was going to be glad to get it all over with. It would be only then that I would be able to sleep well.

At the first hint of dawn I was awake in my room, filling my pipe, watching the day come outside the windows. The trees appeared as black spires against a gray sky first. Then they became green as light filtered down through them. At last I could see the forest floor, glimpse other far more distant trees.

Then I heard movings about, and Anne came by to knock. She was dressed and from the strained look about her face I knew she had not fared any better than I that night.

"I'll start knocking pans around," she said. "That will get everybody up. Who's going to be first?"

"Glenn," I said. My hands shook. I brought them together so she wouldn't see. But she had seen.

"It was a bad night for you too, wasn't it?" Then she started down the hall. Soon I heard the pans downstairs.

I had showered and shaved. Now I brought out my bottle of lotion, but it was all I could do to shake a little out in my hand, put it on my face. Maybe, I reflected, something went wrong at the company. Maybe the stuff's in there right now and when I go out everybody will start screaming. It was a horrible thought. It sent shudders through me. The smell of it actually sickened me as I remembered its effect. But of course it wasn't the doctored lotion.

I dressed, still not feeling any better about it, put on my robe, dropped the lotion in my robe pocket, left the room, went down the hall and knocked on the Klocks' door.

"Just a minute," Lula called out. They were scurrying around inside. In a little while she opened the door.

"Hi," I said. I couldn't for the moment think of anything else to say, standing there, the lotion in the pocket burning a hole there. "Glad to see you're up. Breakfast in a little while."

Lula smiled, held the door wider. "Come on in, Phil. We just got up. What's for breakfast, anyway?"

I came in, saw Glenn come out of the bathroom in his undershirt. He said, "Hi," and reached for a shirt on a chair.

"Hi," I said again. "Can't tell you what's for breakfast. The cook's busy downstairs. Probably heard her, didn't you?"

"We did hear a clatter," she said.

I should have been at ease, but muscles in my back were so taut they ached. My hands were sweaty. My lips were dry and I moistened them with my tongue.

Lula was looking at me curiously. "Anything wrong, Phil?"

"Wrong?" I said heartily. "What could be wrong, Lula? No, it's a beautiful day, we're out in the country, and we're going to have a fine breakfast. What could be wrong with that?"

"I still think you're a lucky guy," Glenn said, buttoning his shirt. "Lula thinks so too. We both think Anne's the greatest."

"She is," I said honestly. I either had to do it now or get out, but I was waging a Civil War in my mind. I hated to do it to Glenn, but I had to. "Say," I said, as if I'd just thought of something. "Ever try this shaving lotion?"

I tossed him the bottle. "Try some, Glenn."

He caught it. He probably would have caught it if it had been dynamite, simply by reflex action.

But what he did with it next was what counted.

He looked at it, unscrewed the stopper, shook a little out in his hand, smelled it. Lula was paying him no attention. Next Glenn spread it over his jowls.

"Not bad," he said. "This the kind you use?"

"Yes," I said. "That's the kind I use."

"You men and your shaving lotions," Lula said. "You're as bad as women and their perfumes."

I let out a weary sigh, sat on the bed.

"There is too something wrong," Lula said, giving me all her attention. "What is it, Phil?"

"So," I said, "it must be Cliff."

"What?" Glenn asked, buttoning the last button. He'd stoppered the bottle, had tossed it to the bed.

I told them how it was. When it was over, Lula was white-faced and shaken. She had collapsed in a chair and sat looking at me dazedly. She turned her eyes to Glenn. "I want to go home," she said. Joy had gone out of her. She was afraid.

"You really think it's Cliff, then?" Glenn asked.

"Who else could it be?"

"And you're going to try the bottle on him?"

"I'll have to."

Glenn turned to Lula. "We've got to go downstairs, Lula. We've got to keep up our end of it."

"I don't want to," Lula said. "I don't want any more of it. I thought if we came up here we'd get away from it all. Now it's come back as bad as ever."

"Lula's nerves," Glenn said. "They're not in the best of shape. This has got her down again."

I said, "Tell you what. Why don't you two stay here? I'll go tackle Cliff. You don't have to be in on it."

Glenn nodded. "Maybe you'd better do that, Phil."

I left them, closed the door behind me, went down the hall. Clifford Ellis's bedroom door stood open. The bed had been made.

108

I was startled, wondered if he had even slept in it. But then I heard voices downstairs. Anne's and Cliff's.

I went down, the bottle once again im my robe. Cliff was in the kitchen with Anne, seated at the kitchen table, smoking a cigarette. He grinned at me.

"Good morning, glory," he said, flicking a little ash in a tray.

"Good morning."

Anne said, "Cliff's been giving me cooking instructions." Her look was an intense one, searching. I could tell her nothing in the glance I returned. She went on, "He says he always gives his girls cooking instructions at breakfast."

"Merely strategy in handling them," Cliff said. "Of course I go only with girls who want to be dominated." Suddenly his eyes narrowed a little. "You don't look so good, Phil."

"I guess not," I said. "I didn't sleep well."

"Why not?"

"Because of this." I withdrew and tossed the bottle to him. As in Glenn's case, he caught it. He put it on the table before him, stared at it.

"What's the gag?" he said, glaring at me.

"Try some," I said. "It's just my after-shave lotion. Think you might like it."

He looked at it. "Not my brand," he said.

I came over to him. "Try it," I said harshly.

"Try it?" He looked at me blankly. "Now why the hell should I do that? I told you, it's not my brand."

Anne said, "Try it for me, then. Phil's just running a comparison test, that's all."

"I'm no guinea pig," Cliff said, drawing on his cigarette. "I don't like people to throw things at me."

"You seem awfully touchy this morning," I said, reaching for the bottle. "Why?"

"You're screwy," Cliff said. "Something's wrong with you. I can't figure it out." He watched me unstopper the bottle. "Now what are you doing?"

I whipped the bottle around, spewing the fluid in his direction. But Cliff didn't move. He just sat there, staring at me. "Phil DeMoss," he said finally, his face speckled with droplets, "have you gone out of your mind?" He sniffed the air. "If it's any comfort to you, I wouldn't have that cheap lotion on a bet." He got out a handkerchief, swabbed his face, glanced down at his shirt and trousers. "Now look what you've done. Got the damn stuff all over. Is that any way to start off the day?"

Suddenly he was on his feet, had grabbed the bottle from my hand. The next thing I knew he was shaking the bottle over my head and most of what was left in it was running past my ears, down my cheeks. It struck me funny and I started to laugh. Then Anne caught it. Finally we were all laughing.

"Hell," Cliff said, putting the bottle back on the kitchen table, "it's too early for games." He fished for another cigarette. "Besides, I didn't think it was that funny. There must have been a joke somewhere and I think it backfired. What was it?"

I told him. When I finished, he said, "I ought to punch you right in the nose for suspecting me."

Anne said, "Well, I guess it must have been a creature from outer space after all."

We finally had breakfast, and things began to get back to normal. Even Lula recovered a little and was able to eat along with the rest of us. Glenn and Cliff were put out with me at first and weren't civil, but Anne smoothed things over by telling them just how we had arrived at our conclusions, and at last they agreed there wasn't much else to think.

"Which leaves us chasing rainbows," Cliff said.

"Nobody outside the Forty-two Club is a victim," Glenn said. "That's what strikes me as odd."

"There are suicides every day," Anne said. "Maybe most of them are caused this way."

Cliff shook his head. "You're trying to make something big out of it. I still think the club—what's left of it—is the prime target."

"But why?" Lula wailed. "Why, why, why?"

I said, "My brain is numb trying to figure it out." It was, too. None of it made sense. If it were only a matter of killing somebody, a simple murder, a bad guy, a good guy, the police chasing the bad guy, that would seem normal. Except none of us was in the bad category. We were all the good guys. And murder wasn't involved. The lotion only aided the victim to do away with himself.

"Jake Hardy was the last to get it," Glenn said. "Now I wonder who's going to be next."

"Yes, Jake called to tell me that. Lieutenant Grever had told me not to mention the lotion to anyone, so I didn't tell Jake. He'd be here if I had. Now he's probably gone too."

Cliff said, "We all ought to be out hunting for Jake instead of horsing around up here."

"Poor Jake," Glenn said.

"Why don't you call Lieutenant Grever?" Anne said. "Maybe they've found him."

I hadn't thought about Jake for some time, so intent had I been on my little experiment.

"He ought to be told about Glenn and Cliff, too," she said. "He ought to know it's no one in the club."

"Yeah," I said wearily. "He'll be glad to hear that. He can start from scratch. Maybe he's got an antidote by this time."

"Let's hope so," Lula said. "I've been living under the threat so long I don't know what it feels like to draw a relaxed breath."

After breakfast I put in the call. Grever was there, and he wasn't happy when I told him where we were.

"You should have kept in touch," he growled. "Something might have come up."

"I'm sorry," I said. "We forgot to."

"Well, I knew you were there, I got the phone number from Mrs. Whiting two hours ago. I was going to call, but there was no hurry. We still haven't analyzed the stuff, but they're working on it."

I told him what Anne and I had done. Grever muttered something unprintable. "I hope," he said, "you didn't bungle it."

"I didn't bungle it. They couldn't possibly be guilty. I'd be willing to bet my life on that."

"Well, if that's true it solves the case."

"Solves the case?" I was baffled.

"Sure. You could have saved yourself time and effort if you had kept in touch instead of gallivanting all over the countryside with a lotion bottle."

"You've lost me somewhere, Lieutenant."

"Have I? Do you remember your telling me you'd been called by Jake Hardy? You said he had this thing, that he'd left his house."

"Sure. Did they ever find him?"

"Sure they did."

"Was he still alive?"

"Very much alive. Right after you called, I got in touch with the sheriff. He sent some men out to Jake's house."

"He shouldn't have done that. Jake wasn't there."

"That's right. Want to know where they found him?"

"Where?"

"At the municipal water plant."

"At the plant?" Now why should Jake have gone to the water-works under the influence of a thing like that?

"Yep. At the plant. He was very healthy. Very much alive. Does that suggest anything to you?"

"You mean he wasn't affected by this thing?"

"Of course. He lied to you and it made me out a fool, sending those deputies out there on a wild goose chase. Mr. Hardy was considerably put out that he'd been reported missing or the victim of anything. So it wasn't Jake Hardy who called you."

"It was. He's the guilty man, Lieutenant."

"Think so? I'm not so sure."

"You've got to pick him up, Lieutenant."

"Pick him up?" Grever laughed. "I can't pick him up on your say-so. Besides, San Benuto is out of my territory. I might ask the county authorities to do it, but before I'd do that I'd have to have some proof he is the guilty one."

"He's the only one left!"

"This little elimination game of yours might satisfy you, Mr. DeMoss, but it will take a little more than that to satisfy me and the sheriff."

FIFTEEN

When I put the telephone back on its hook on the wall, it was the only sound in the room. I turned around to look into the faces of my weekend companions. Anne was standing by the fireplace, her eyes questioning, asking me what I was going to do now. Cliff was sitting in an overstuffed chair, one arm over the side of it, smoke trailing up his fingers from a cigarette. He was scowling at me. The Klocks were sitting together on one part of a sectional sofa and Glenn had clasped one of her hands in his. They were looking at me too, Glenn a little outraged and at the same time bewildered, Lula frightened again.

There was no need to tell them what had been said. They'd heard my side of it. They could fill in the missing parts. If they were thinking what I was, then they knew who the guilty one was, the man who had sent three of our numbers to their deaths.

They were thinking too there was nothing any of us could do about it. If Grever can't do anything, what can we do?

"So it was Jake," Glenn said softly. Lula moved closer.

"Looks that way," I said.

Cliff swore and looked at the floor. Nobody minded.

Anne said, "Why can't Lieutenant Grever have him arrested? If he's the one, why should he be free to carry on? Look at the horror he has already caused."

"That's easy to say, Anne," I said quietly, moving away from the phone and sinking into a straight chair.

"What do you mean, 'That's easy to say'?" Cliff asked.

"We don't really *know* he's the one," I said.

"Oh, come on, Phil, he's got to be. Who's left?"

"Nobody, I suppose."

"You're the legal eagle. How could it be done?"

"No way. Oh, he could be picked up, held twenty-four or forty-eight hours maybe. But what good would that do?"

"If I were Grever," Cliff said grimly, "I'd get it out of him. There's just that much sadism in me for men of his type. It would be a pleasure, considering what he's done."

I glared at him. "This isn't a witch-hunt, Cliff."

"If you ask me—but you'd better not—I've got a worse word than that for it."

"And it isn't the Middle Ages."

Cliff grinned sourly. "Hamstrung by our own laws."

"You're assuming too much," I told him.

"Am I? Just what am I assuming, Phil?"

"You're assuming his guilt."

"And you're defending him?"

"In order to hold Jake it would have to be proved that he planted that stuff in bottles of shaving lotion at three places, not counting my own. Poley McGowan's house, Ernst Mollinauer's and Herb Lincoln's. I feel pretty sure he managed to get into the McGowan house and into Mollinauer's apartment as he did mine, by merely visiting. I don't know. I couldn't prove it. But he broke into Herb Lincoln's house. One of the windows had been jimmied. Lieutenant Grever was supposed to send some men out to try to lift prints from there. I don't know that he ever did.

"It would also have to be pretty well proved that Jake knew what the new ingredient in the lotion would do, that it was a premeditated thing. We would have to show that it would drive those unfamiliar with it to suicide—or at the very least expose them to danger. Ane what kind of charge would we arrest Jake on, presuming that we had proved all the foregoing facts? The lotion itself isn't dangerous. If you are familiar with it, you need not expose yourself to any danger or discomfort at all."

"Great, Counsellor DeMoss," Cliff said wryly, clapping his hands. "What you are saying is that a person need not use the lotion at all. If he doesn't use it, he's in no danger."

I nodded. "Unfortunately, that's true. I'm not so sure but what that Jake could get off the hook if his lawyer were on his toes."

"If he argued as you do," Cliff said.

Glenn said, "Would you take his case, Phil?"

"No," I said. "I certainly would not. Not after what has happened. But I do know lawyers who would."

"All this arguing," Anne said. "And we don't even know that Jake is in fact guilty. It's ironic—think of it. He could be as innocent as any of us."

"No, Anne. I don't believe that. He *did* call me. I remember how surprised he was to hear my voice. He planted the stuff Wednesday night, and he was calling me to find out if I had by any chance returned home, since I hadn't been located by Grever or you three who had carried on a search for me. No wonder he talked in such an odd way! Getting me like that was unexpected, and for a moment he was rattled. So he made up the story that he had become a victim. That would throw me off the track—or it would make him a brother in misery. And if I had discovered anything I would be apt to tell him, warn him. But Lieutenant Grever had asked me not to reveal what we had discovered, so I didn't tell him, and Jake was emboldened by it, thinking I'd get a dose of it again the next morning. Jake knows me. He knew I wouldn't be able to stay in the house. Or at least he hoped so. As long as I didn't know what caused it, there was always the chance I'd end up like Poley or Ernst or Herb. He was counting on it. He knew I would be worried about myself and not about him. He probably chuckled when I told him to stay home. He chuckled and went right down to the waterworks."

Cliff said, "That's right. If he had it, really had it, he would have called me. He was always calling me about something." He put out his cigarette in a tray at the side of the chair. "He is a lonely man. His whole life is those pipes down there at the waterworks. He's there more than he's at home, works all the odd shifts."

"I just can't feature his doing it," Glenn said. "A few minutes ago I felt pretty sure it had to be Jake. Now I don't know."

"Why?" I asked.

Glenn looked at me squarely. "At one time you were pretty sure it was either Cliff or me."

"Well," I said lamely, "I won't deny that."

"And it might not have been Jake who called you," Lula said.

"Oh, it was Jake all right. I'd know Jake's voice."

"Small minds, small chatter," Cliff said, lighting another cigarette. "It appears as usual that I'm the only one with any sense."

"What," I said, borrowing his technique, "is your giant brain telling you?"

He shrugged. "It isn't the size of the brain that counts, Phil. It's how you use it."

Lula said, "When do you start?"

"No need to start. I've just finished."

"Well, what is it?" I asked in an exasperated voice.

"It's simple. Throw the bottle of lotion at Jake Hardy just as you did at us. Could anything be simpler?"

We all sat there looking at him, each of us trying to find something wrong with it. The only thing wrong was that there was

114

nothing wrong with it. I hated to admit it, especially verbally. But Anne did.

She said, "Cliff's right. That would prove it."

Glenn said something about how it probably would, and Lula said nothing at all.

Cliff expanded on it. "Look, I know Jake better than any of you. It's Sunday and I know he'll be at the plant. Nobody else around." His eyes snapped brightly. "And I've been sitting here thinking about that very thing and I think I've got the answer. Who has time to experiment with this sort of thing? Nobody but Jake. Why does he so unselfishly work the odd shifts—at least the weekend ones? Why, so that he can fiddle around at the plant.

"I've been there, in the plant, I mean, many times. He's got a chemical laboratory—of course all water plants need laboratories for water testing. But unless I'm wrong, it seems to me that this is a little more than an ordinary, simple water-testing laboratory. That is the thing that has been stuck in my head and now I know that he's our man. He's been working weekends for a long time. I never knew why, but now I know. It was so he could kill Poley and Ernst and Herb and the rest of us."

"But why would he want to do that?" Anne asked. "You say you know him so well. Tell us why."

Cliff shook his head soberly. "I don't know. All I know is I have suddenly come to hate this man. I always knew he had a petty mind. Sometimes I have thought it was a filthy mind. But I always accepted him for what he is. But this, this I find I cannot accept. I cannot accept it because I remember Poley and Ernst and Herb too well. I know you will think it out of character of me to say so, but I want to say I think they were three of the finest guys in the world." He cocked an eye at me. "And if you'd got yours in that alley you talked about, I'd say the same thing about you."

We were quiet for a while. Then I said, "I guess I'd better get on down to San Benuto with the lotion bottle."

"I think we'd all better go down," Cliff said. "I want to be in on the finish of this thing. And if Jake so much as bats an eye at the bottle, I think I'll clobber him."

That was enough for me, and we all started to get ready to leave. All except Lula. She stood by, wringing her hands, saying, "I won't go," in a scarcely audible voice.

Glenn went to her, but she only repeated in a louder voice, "I won't go, Glenn. I don't want any more of it. I don't want to see Jake. I just want to go home."

"Honey," he said, taking her hand, "Phil and Cliff may need

help. I can't just let them walk in on Jake like this. Maybe Jake will get violent or something. Nobody can tell about things like that."

"That's what I mean," she said. "Violence. I don't want any more violence. Why don't you just get him arrested? Why should you risk your life doing something the police are paid to do?" She pressed herself against him. "Let them go, Glenn. I don't want you to."

Glenn detached her from him, said firmly, "I've got to go, Lula. I've got to do it for Poley and Ernst and Herb. Don't you see?"

"All right," she said. "All right, Glenn."

In a matter of minutes we were five people in three cars on the way to San Benuto. Because my car was the oldest I was in the lead with Anne at my side. Behind us was Glenn and Lula Klock, with Cliff alone in his Corvette. Once again it was a beautiful day and I felt real regret that we weren't able to stay at the Whiting hideaway. It would have been wonderful. But there would be other days, other times. Days and times when this threat no longer hung over us, days and times of normality, when we'd think and talk about the world situation, the baseball leagues, best sellers and what's new on TV.

"I don't mind telling you," Anne said, "I'm scared. My palms are dripping water."

"Why?" As if I didn't know.

"Lula's talk about not wanting violence. I don't either, and I'm afraid there will be."

"There won't be any," I said with conviction I didn't feel. "Five against one. Or, reducing it to men, three against one. But I don't think there'll be anything to it."

"But if you face him with it . . ." She let it trail off.

"So we face him with it. I toss him the bottle. He reacts. We've got him or we haven't."

"If you get him, he'll be a cornered man, desperate."

"We're not the police, Anne. Of course we could make a citizen's arrest, but I don't think we'll need to do anything like that."

"What will you do?"

My mind hadn't dwelt on it, but I had considered it. I said, "Make him talk. Convince him he ought to go to the police with it. That's all."

For a long time Anne didn't say anything. She just sat there, hunched down in her seat, looking out the window. Finally, she said, "Well, I'm still scared."

"Maybe we all are," I conceded. "It's no picnic we're going to.

I know I feel on edge. But I'm trying not to let it get me down."

A few miles this side of San Benuto, Glenn Klock pulled on ahead of me and then signalled for me to slow down and stop behind him. I did; he got out, came back to my car, and Cliff came up from his.

"Phil," Glenn said, "I've got to take Lula home. She's going off the deep end again. Doesn't want me to see Jake."

That was bad, but it couldn't be helped. I couldn't ask a man to break up his happy home. I said, "Maybe you'd better go on home then, Glenn."

"I hate to do it. I know how much you guys might need me there. But Lula's scared to death."

Cliff laid a hand on his shoulder. "You go ahead, Glenn. We'll handle it." He sounded very optimistic. I wished I felt that way. Cliff went on, "We'll give you a ring when it's all over."

Glenn looked at the ground and said, "I still hate to do it."

"Go on," I said. "Lula needs you more than we do, Glenn."

"O.K." He looked at Cliff, then at me. "You guys be careful."

"We'll be all of that," I said.

Then we were on our way again, and Anne said, "What did you say the odds were?"

"Just like at the track," I said. "The odds go down before the big race."

"That should mean something," she said.

San Benuto is one of those pretty California towns in open country between mountains: clean streets, bright pastel houses, and carefully tended lawns. The waterworks was on the east side in an older section of town, but there was nothing old about the low-slung structure that could have been put up no less than ten years ago. It was surrounded by a wire fence covered with ivy, and there were flower beds running the entire length of the building at the front. I caught a glimpse of a near-ground-level reservoir behind the main building as we drove up. It was circular and looked more like a swimming pool, but there were no diving boards. Only aerators, I guessed. Or whatever the pipes were that stuck out of it.

We parked in the area before the main building, walked up the white sidewalk, found the office door locked. Of course it would be, considering it was Sunday. We three walked around the building with its glass brick windows to the rear. Here there were flower beds, too, and lawns, and the main door at the rear had been propped open. A bicycle lay on the sidewalk and there were voices inside.

We walked in. Jake Hardy was stooped over a workbench.

At his side stood a boy, a youngster not quite yet in his teens. They were engrossed with whatever was on the bench.

Jake heard our steps, turned and saw us. He straightened, showed his big white teeth in a smile, reached up a forefinger and smoothed his mustache. "I'll be darned," he said in pleasant surprise.

The boy turned and looked at us with hostile eyes.

"I will be darned," Jake said again, moving away from the bench a little. He shook his head. "After all these years and finally somebody comes around. Come on in and sit down."

The boy tripped us up. All the things I had wanted to say right from the beginning couldn't be said now with the boy there. I glanced at the workbench, saw a water pistol there. A large plastic thing, semitransparent. Around it lay screwdrivers, electrician's tape and a tube of what looked like solvent.

Jake saw where I was looking, picked up the pistol. "This is Ernie Bush. Friend of mine. Where else would you go to get a plugged-up water pistol fixed but at the waterworks, eh, Ernie?"

Ernie smiled a little, but he was still put out because we had interrupted work on the pistol.

"These are friends of mine," Jake went on. "Maybe you'd better run along, Ernie. We'll finish the job later."

"Ain't you done yet?" Ernie said.

"Not quite. You go ahead. You can pick it up some other time. This afternoon maybe."

Ernie Bush gave us all a glare and walked out to his bike.

"Well, Prez," Jake said, nodding at me. Then Anne, "Miss Whiting," and Cliff. "Grab a chair."

"We won't be sitting down, Jake," I said. "We want to talk to you about something. We'd prefer to stand."

"Well, sure. Go ahead." There was puzzlement in his eyes. Real or faked. But it was there. "What is it?"

I found enough breath to say, "We're going to talk about what you did to Poley, Ernst and Herb. We're going to talk about how you drove the first two to suicide, the last one to his death on the street."

Jake stood there with a blank look. Then he felt for and sat on a high stool near the bench, still staring. At last he said, "You think I had anything to do with that?"

Cliff said, "Jake, you had everything to do with it. You had the time, you have the lab. Why don't you just tell us all about it?"

Jake shook his head. "I don't know what to say."

Anne said, "You could say the truth."

"Miss Whiting," Jake said, "do you think I had anything to do with all this?"

"Jake," I said, "you said you had this thing that Poley and Ernst had. When the deputies came looking for you, you were here at the plant. You couldn't have had it."

"So you had something to do with those men coming here!" He got to his feet. "If you don't think that was crazy, those deputies coming around! Did you send them?"

"I didn't send them. Lieutenant Grever did. I called him after you called me, and he in turn called the sheriff's office."

"I called you?" Jake said, bewildered. "When did I call you?"

"The day before yesterday," I snapped. "Don't try to tell me it wasn't you who called."

"But I never called you, Phil!"

"You called me because you and Glenn and Cliff were out looking for me the night before. You wanted to find out if I was still among the living, and you were surprised to find that I was."

"You're way off base, Phil. I never called you at all."

"I told you I had it, you said you had it too. I told you to stay home so you wouldn't get hurt. You asked me to contact Grever for you."

"Phil, Phil, you're all wrong, you're barking up the wrong tree. I didn't have anything to do with this. Somebody's trying to put something over on you." He narrowed his eyes, looked at Cliff. "Cliff, I thought you were a friend of mine. Do you believe what Phil's saying?"

"It seems reasonable," Cliff said.

Jake looked beyond us. "Where's Glenn? He ought to be here. He'd believe me. Somebody's got to. This is all wrong."

I thought we'd played it out far enough. I reached into my pocket, brought out the bottle of lotion.

"Here," I said, tossing it to him.

Jake caught it.

SIXTEEN

If there was any doubt about Jake's guilt—and the room was full of it right then—it evaporated when we all saw the look on his face when he saw what he had caught. He didn't have eyes for us any more; they were on the bottle and they grew larger the longer he looked at it. His mustache seemed to turn jet black, but it was only because his face was so quickly drained of its color.

Jake set the bottle on the workbench beside the water gun. He set it there gingerly, carefully. Then he turned to us. He

119

swallowed, wet his lips, tried to smile. He was making a real effort to get control of himself.

"Thanks," he said. "Just what I've always wanted." His voice wasn't the usual Jake Hardy voice. How could it be?

"Sort of got you, didn't it?" Cliff said.

"I didn't expect any gifts," Jake said, recovering a little.

"It isn't a gift," I said, moving toward the workbench. Jake watched me fascinatedly as I picked up the bottle. He blanched even more as I carefully unscrewed the top, handling it as if it were something that would explode at the slightest jar. "Here, take a little on the palm of your hand," I said, extending the bottle.

"No," he said, backing away. "I don't think I need any." Again he licked his dry lips.

We locked eyes, Jake and I, and he retreated at my advance. "Why not, Jake? It's only the lotion that was in my medicine cabinet. Don't you want to try a little of it?"

We had travelled halfway across the room. Now Jake's buttocks were against a table there. No place else to go.

Jake said, "I—I don't like smelly stuff like that."

"Take some," I said. Suddenly I swung the bottle out in an arc and droplets went sailing through the air toward him.

Jake screamed, ducked out of the way. Some of the lotion landed on his face nonetheless and he started pawing at it with his hands. As suddenly as he started to try to remove it, he stopped and straightened to look at us.

We stared back.

Then his shoulders slumped. "A trick, wasn't it?"

"Yes, it was a trick, Jake. It's not the same bottle as the one you put the stuff in."

Now he went to the workbench, picked up a pack of cigarettes there, fished one out, lit it, and sank to the stool, staring at the floor. Cliff said something under his breath and started for Jake, but he stopped halfway to him and I knew why. Jake was the picture of dejection. He didn't seem to care what happened, whether or not Cliff said or did anything. I almost felt sorry for him.

"Why did you do it, Jake?" Cliff said. "Why in hell did you do it?"

Jake's eyes came up. They were resigned eyes, eyes empty of challenge, empty of hope. "It was a joke," he said.

"A joke!" Cliff could hardly contain himself. "A fine joke on Poley and Ernst and Herb, Jake. A fine joke for three dead men."

"Don't you suppose I know it's not a joke—*now?*" Jake was a tormented man. God only knows what nightmares he must have lived through in his mind the past weeks.

120

"You were always a practical joker," I said. "This time you went too far, is that what you're trying to tell us?"

Jake looked at his hands, picked up the water pistol and fiddled with it, saying, "I thought it would be a big joke. I've got a lot of them. Like this water pistol here. I gave it to Ernie." He paused, then went on rapidly, "He's got a big sister and he gets even with her by squirting her with it. He's told me about it. It's funny. I could tell you some funny things that have happened with it."

"Tell us what funny things happened with the stuff you put in the lotion bottles," Cliff said. "Tell us so we can laugh, too."

Jake said miserably, "I know it isn't funny. I was monkeying around with a lot of things here in the lab. One day I ran across some stuff that I happened to get on my hand. It about scared Ernie to death when he came to see me. I tried it out on some of the others who work here. There's a girl, a bookkeeper——"

"I suppose you mean Miss Enright?" Cliff said.

"Yeah. I forgot you know her. I diluted the stuff down, spilled a little on her by accident, but of course it wasn't an accident. Well, you know Miss Enright. Always talking, gossiping, never gets any work done."' A faint smile crossed Jake's face. "That day nobody'd listen to her. She doesn't know to this day what was wrong with her. Of course it was real weak, that stuff."

"You thought you'd strengthen it a little for Poley, though. Is that right?"

"Cliff, I just did it for kicks, believe me. Poley liked to talk so big. Him and Ernst. They were a pair. Biggest talkers. Big 'I' men. All that money, lording it over the rest of us at the annual meeting. Oh, I didn't mind it, but I thought it would be funny if they should suddenly be not so popular, see how things look from the other side of the fence."

I said, "So you paid them a visit and put some in their shaving lotion."

He nodded. "That way I'd be sure only they'd get it. Poley's lotion was about half gone. I went to his place on a Sunday night, early. Later on I dropped in on Ernst. Ernst had two bottles. One nearly empty, the other full. I didn't want to put anything in the nearly empty bottle because it would have been too strong, so I put it in the nearly full bottle for the right dilution."

"Both on the same night?"

"Yeah. Ernst had to use up the nearly empty bottle first. That's why there was a time lag." He put out his cigarette, got tired of playing with the water gun and put it back on the bench.

"Then you sat back and waited," I said.

"Yeah. But I didn't think it would be that bad. Oh, I knew something would happen, but I didn't think it would kill anybody. I kept waiting to hear, but nothing happened for a whole week. Then I heard Poley walked into the ocean." His eyes came up. They wanted us to believe him. "I didn't connect that and the lotion at first. I thought he'd committed suicide, just as everybody else did. But then I got to thinking about it. Then I knew what I'd done."

Cliff snorted. "You were real sorry, I bet. I bet you laughed yourself silly when you heard about it."

"Please," Jake said. "I didn't think it was funny at all."

"Go on," I said gently.

"You could have got the bottle out of Ernst's place," Cliff said. "Why didn't you do that?"

"I didn't think about it. All I could think of is what I did to Poley. I—I got drunk. I stayed that way for days."

"A fine escape," Cliff said. "Everybody was unhappy but you. You were off on an alcoholic kick."

"And when I did think about the bottle in Ernst's place I didn't know what to do. If I told anybody about it, I'd get blamed for Poley's death."

"You thought more of yourself than you did Ernst," Cliff went on mercilessly. "Is that what you're trying to tell us?"

"No. I was scared. I couldn't say anything."

"It's a wonder you didn't get drunk again."

"I did, I did." Jake was practically beside himself with agony, and tears were beginning to form. "I drank until I couldn't think about it any more. And then the next thing I read was where Ernst—where Ernst died."

"Where your friend Ernst jumped from his bedroom window because of what you did to him, you mean," Cliff said. "It was just as if you pushed him, Jake. Pushed him out that window with all your might."

"I couldn't help it," Jake cried. "I couldn't help it, I tell you. I tried to think of a way to get back into the house, but I couldn't. I couldn't face him or Rose. I just couldn't. They'd be able to tell something was wrong." Jake brought out a handkerchief and dabbed at his eyes. "I just couldn't bring myself to do it, Cliff."

"You could have taken one of us into your confidence. I would have gone after that bottle. Phil here would have. You might have even told Ernst about it. Maybe he would have forgiven you if you had."

"I thought about all that."

"You didn't think enough about it, Jake. You thought maybe a little about everybody else, but a lot about yourself. You figured you could play the thing out to the end. You thought you'd get your kicks out of even more of it."

"No," Jake said fiercely. "That's not true. After Ernst died I didn't know what to do. I even thought of committing suicide. I couldn't look myself in the eye. I mean it, Cliff."

"Sure, Jake."

"Jake," I said, "What about Herb Lincoln?"

"That's the worst part, Phil. Positively the worst. I found out you and Herb were working on it, that Herb was getting close. I had to get rid of him. By that time I was in over my head. I couldn't let anybody find out about it or I would be arrested like a common criminal. I didn't know whether to tell him about it and throw myself on his mercy or to try to get rid of him. I thought if the same thing happened to him, maybe he'd commit suicide and then I wouldn't have anything to worry about; but it backfired."

I said, "You broke into his place."

"Yes, I broke in. I put it into a lotion bottle. And then he figured it out. I didn't know what to do."

"How do you know he figured it out?" I asked.

"I called him. I kept bothering him. And in the middle of one of the calls he accused me of it. He said he was going to turn me over to the police unless I told him what was in the solution I put in the lotion bottle. I told him he was crazy—what else could I do? I couldn't tell him everything."

"I don't think he really thought you were the one," I said. "He never mentioned it anyway."

"He was killed on the way to the hospital to analyze it," Cliff said. "If you had told him, he'd be alive today. He would have had no need to go to the hospital."

Then I said, "I was next."

Jake nodded dumbly. "Yes." He sighed. "You were next. I put it into your lotion that night at the meeting. You were getting too close for comfort."

"It got easier and easier, didn't it?" Cliff said. "First Poley, and that was the hardest. Then Ernst, and that was a little easier. Then Herb and finally Phil. Only by that time things were beginning to close in. Were you going to get rid of the rest of us? Were you going to get rid of Lieutenant Grever and the whole Los Angeles Police Department and the sheriff's office?"

"No," Jake said wearily. "No. I knew it would end like this, somebody walking in here some day and saying what you're saying."

"A fine picture of a man you are," Cliff went on. "A trusted friend, club member, classmate. All the clichés in the book. And you're none of them. Just a hulk of a man, a wreck of a human being. Why, I doubt there's a spark of humanity in you."

"All right," Jake said. "I'm all of that. But please, Cliff, no more. I can't take any more."

"You're going to have to take plenty more, Jake. You're going to come along with us to the sheriff's office and repeat everything you've told us. Then maybe they'll run you down to Los Angeles and you can do it all over again for Lieutenant Grever."

"All right. Anything you say. I'm just glad it's all over. I'll have to go in and call Andy; he'll have to come out to the plant." He sighed again. "Andy won't like it, but he'll have to." He got up wearily from the stool and walked slowly to a rear room. We could hear the sound of dialing and presently we heard him talking to Andy.

Cliff lit a cigarette with a shaking hand. I brought out my pipe. Cliff said, "Well, looks as if it's all over."

"You were pretty tough on him." I punched tobacco down in the bowl and lit it.

Anne tugged at my sleeve. She'd been standing at my side through it all. Now I turned to her. She was pointing to the workbench. I couldn't see what she meant and said so.

"The water gun," she said. "It's gone."

"So what?" Cliff said. "He's probably got it in his pocket."

"No," she said, looking anxiously toward the room Jake was phoning from. "There's something wrong." She flashed me a glance and I felt it too. "Intuition," she added. We could no longer hear Jake talking. We all thought of it at once, but we didn't have time to step toward the room, which was only fifteen feet away, because at that moment Jake stepped out, the water gun in his hands. He was smiling now and there was a kind of madness about the eyes.

"Ernie's pistol," he said calmly. "Harmless little thing, isn't it? Only right now it's filled with a concentrate. No diluted lotion. And, do you know? This little gun can reach a hundred feet, with the right trajectory, of course. I know because Ernie and I have worked with it. It won't be necessary to shoot it that far, though, since you're all so close."

Cliff wasn't afraid. At least he didn't look afraid. I know I didn't want anything like that squirted on me. Diluted, it was bad enough. Concentrated, it was too much to try to think about. Cliff hadn't gone through what I had. That's why he was able to walk toward him and say, "Let me have that gun. There's no sense in compounding trouble, Jake."

"Stop right there," Jake said. Cliff stopped. Jake went on, "I suppose you think it's easy for me to do this. Believe me, I don't want to. But you've all been so inquisitive, you've all been so nice to me—especially you, Cliff, all those things you said—it's

124

not going to be so hard. Nobody will know what happened to you three. You'll go out the door like shots. It will be funny to watch. Or maybe you'll kill each other. I don't know. Anyway, the reaction, whatever it is, will be amusing indeed."

"You *are* mad," Cliff said.

"Only self-protective, Cliff. That's all. Wouldn't you do the same thing? No jail for me. No. Not for Jake Hardy."

"You can't do it," I said with a calmness I didn't feel. "There's Glenn. He knows about it. He's probably called Lieutenant Grever by this time."

"I'll get Glenn, too. And Lula. She can dance some of those fancy steps of hers first. And it will be a pleasure to see Lieutenant Grever squirm."

"You'll never do it," Cliff said, starting toward him again, "because I'm going to take that gun." I was filled with the heroic aspect of Clifford Ellis at that moment. But I was filled with fear for him too. He just didn't know . . .

"Cliff!" Anne cried, taking a step to stop him.

Jake's smile broadened to a grin. He squeezed the trigger and we all ducked away from where the spray would come.

But no spray came. At least none came from the front end of the gun. A stream of yellow liquid shot instead into the astonished face of Jake Hardy. It squirted from the rear of the gun at the handle where he had taped it, where it was encrusted with plastic solvent.

For a moment he stood transfixed, the solution dotting his forehead, his eyes, nose and cheeks. Then he let out a bellow, grabbed at his eyes as if to tear them from their sockets, gnashed his teeth and made a horrible face. The gun clattered to the floor. He hunched over, ran toward us, screaming shrilly, hitting the stool and staggering off to fall over a chair.

At the same time the room became filled with a vapor that sent us reeling, watering our eyes, convulsing our muscles.

Jake's cries were inhuman as he got to his feet and, with a last piercing scream, ran out of the room. He went out the door which to me now was only a fuzzy rectangle at the end of the room, for the vapor was making me more dizzy, blurring my vision. I fell to the floor, filled with the most violent hatred for everything, yet knowing this was only the reaction, hoping as I struggled for breath and reason, that I could reach that door and go through it.

A few minutes later I crawled through the door, drew in great gulps of fresh air, and lay on the sidewalk thinking of nothing but that I would live, I was safe, remembering nothing, only the horror of the moments just past. I recovered a little, sat up to see Anne sitting dazedly on the lawn, her handkerchief to her eyes, sobbing. Cliff was stretched out on his back, breathing fast to dispel the last of the poison air in his lungs. He was staring stupidly at the sky. His lips were working, but he was making no sound.

A little later I managed to find my voice. "Anne," I said. "Anne." She stopped sobbing and took the handkerchief from her eyes. Then she turned her head slowly and saw me.

"Oh, Phil!" she said. Then she was sobbing again.

I tried to get up, but things started to shift sidewise when I did, so I stayed down, crawled to her. I took her by the shoulders and held her close, let her sob her heart out.

Cliff eventually stopped gasping for breath and turned his head to watch us. His eyes were vacant at first, but they gradually focused and there was reason in them again.

"God, Phil," he said. That seemed to tax him, so he lay there for a long time before he said, "That was terrible." Then he found he could sit up.

A red-haired man came around the corner of the building at that moment, a man busy with his arms and feet in getting somewhere and knowing just where: the door of the building. But he stopped so short that he nearly toppled when he saw us. His eyes popped out and his mouth dropped open. Then his nose made like a rabbit's and I knew that the vapor, what little of it there was out here, had come to him.

"You're Andy," I said.

"Andy Gerling. That's right. Who might you people be?"

How could we tell him? We just sat there.

"Where's Jake?" He looked beyond us, around us, took a step to the door.

"Better not go in," I said. "Jake's not in there, and besides . . ." I sighed and got to my feet, helped Anne to hers. I felt beat. I could tell that Anne didn't feel any better.

Now the eyes were no longer popeyes. They were heavy-lidded and suspicious. "Who're you people? What are you doing here?"

Cliff looked around. "We'd better find Jake." He turned to Andy. "You'd better help. Jake ran out of there a little while ago. He's in trouble." He went on to explain a little of it and I filled in when he ran out of breath. It wasn't much, but I think we got the point across because Andy started up the gentle rise that ran to the reservoir.

I knew then why we hadn't heard Jake's cries any more.

Anne didn't come with us. Just Cliff and Andy and I. We walked to the reservoir. Face down in the water was Jake Hardy, spread-eagled. And quiet. There was a brilliant red line across the back of his neck where some of the liquid had run.

126

Suddenly I hated Jake Hardy. Hated the water. I found myself wanting to destroy something. We all must have felt it because we turned as one man and walked back to the building again, Cliff talking agitatedly to Andy.

When Anne looked at me questioningly, I said, "He's in the water," and I took her arm. She moved close to me and we walked together along the bright walk beside the building. The sun was warm.

"Poor Jake," she said. "But I think he would have rather had it end this way."

"Poley, Ernst and Herb, too. Nothing long and drawn out."

"I have a feeling they might have even understood Jake."

"Maybe they would have forgiven him. They were that kind of men, Anne."

She squeezed my hand. "So are you, Phil."

I began to feel better. About everything.

It was like coming out of a long, dark tunnel.

If you have enjoyed this book and wish to have a complete, free list of Sphere Books, please write to

Sphere
40 Park Street
London W.1.